Karnes
302 Parkway Dr.

Illustrated by Leonard Shortall

WEEKLY READER CHILDRENS BOOK CLUB
Presents

The Curious
Clubhouse

CHRISTINE GOVAN

THE WORLD PUBLISHING COMPANY

CLEVELAND AND NEW YORK

To E. D. W.

who collects cigar boxes, teddy bears, comic books, rags, ribbons, soap coupons, box tops, broken plastic, nails, feathers, Barbie dolls and doll clothes, canceled checks, paper plates, old candles, "string too short to be saved," campaign buttons, voodoo material, pocketbooks, marbles and old stones, medicine bottles, yarn, candy wrappers, and any other objects she may some day have use for—this book is lovingly dedicated.

Published by The World Publishing Company
2231 West 110th Street, Cleveland, Ohio 44102
Published simultaneously in Canada by
Nelson, Foster & Scott Ltd.
Library of Congress catalog card number: 67-23344
Text copyright © 1967 by Christine Govan
Illustrations copyright © 1967 by Leonard Shortall
WP
Designed by Jack Jaget
Weekly Reader Childrens Book Club Edition
Senior Division

THE CURIOUS CLUBHOUSE

1 🌿   Afterward George would always remember that it was a Thursday when they decided to have the clubhouse. Thursday, George thought, was a lucky day because it was the day right before Friday, the last day of school. This Thursday was especially lucky because there was no school. It was the week before summer vacation and the teachers were all busy making out report cards.

Then, too, George and his family were having French toast for breakfast.

Mrs. Carpenter, George's mother, had asked her family to choose one breakfast for each day in the week because she said fixing four different breakfasts each morning was making a skizzofreenic, or something like that, out of her.

Mr. Carpenter had typed the weekly menu and it was pasted on the refrigerator door:

MONDAY:	Scrambled eggs (Karen)
TUESDAY:	Fried eggs and bacon (Daddy)
WEDNESDAY:	Sausage and grits—and I hope, fried apples (George)
THURSDAY:	French toast (Everybody)
FRIDAY:	Poached eggs and toast (Mother)
SATURDAY:	Every man for himself (which usually meant cold cereal and a banana)
SUNDAY:	Something special like fish cakes (if you like fish cakes) and marmalade and hot muffins
EVERY DAY:	Coffee, milk, orange juice.

Fortunately, George liked milk, although Karen was always saying that her best friend, Monica Raney, was allowed coffee for breakfast.

"Crud," said George scornfully when Karen had brought this up again on Thursday morning for about the millionth time. "Milk with a little coffee in it. Baby stuff. I'd rather wait until I can have the real thing."

"George," said his mother. "I have asked you not to use that awful word!"

"What word?" asked George, licking off his milk mustache.

" 'Crud.' And use your napkin."

George was eleven, and his sister, Karen, was ten. She wasn't bad for a girl. She had a short reddish curly bob and blue eyes and freckles. She could ride a bike and swim and climb trees.

Mr. and Mrs. Carpenter were just like all parents— if you know what I mean. Mr. Carpenter had red hair and a short nose and wore glasses. Mrs. Carpenter was short and blond and looked worried a lot of the time, but she was really a good sport. Like the time Awful Prentice left his chewing gum on the cookout grill and Mr. Carpenter put the steak on it. Awful's name was really Orville but he did such wild things all the time that everybody called him Awful.

Well, the entire Carpenter family was eating French toast on the screened porch off the kitchen and Mrs. Carpenter said, "Karen, before you do anything else this morning you have got to tidy up your room. And I mean really tidy it up. All those movie magazines, those cardboard boxes, that collection of bears and box tops have got to be put away neatly, or out they go."

"Not my bears!" wailed Karen. She'd had this collection of big stuffed bears and silly little doll bears ever since she was six years old. She had a dollhouse for the small bears and rode them around in wagons made out of match boxes. They had wrecks and all had to go to the hospital with broken legs and all that. She was too big to play with them and she got as mad as spit if any of the older girls found out about them. But she wouldn't give them up.

"Let's have a big bear funeral," said George, who was always full of good ideas. "We can bear-y them in the straw-beary bed!"

This was so funny he choked on his milk. Mrs. Carpenter gave him a look and Mr. Carpenter said, "For Pete's sake, wipe your face!"

"And Karen," went on Mrs. Carpenter, "that paint box and glass of water in the middle of the living room floor—the puzzle on the window seat—the book you left outdoors all night and that might be ruined—all those and any other things you have left out must be picked up and put away—neatly—not stuffed under your bed. Do you hear me?"

Karen nodded glumly.

"And George—you left your bicycle right in front of the steps last night. If anyone had come to call, he might have fallen over it. And that model airplane you're making—get it out of the living room. Your bathing suit is still dripping in the bathroom and your tennis shoes are by the sink."

Mr. Carpenter held out his cup and she poured him some more coffee. But that didn't stop her. She went right on.

"And I have seven socks in the wash. Look under your bed and behind the bureau and around the house until you find the eighth one. I just bought them last month and I don't intend to buy any more."

George couldn't care less about socks. Socks were just a nuisance anyway in hot weather. He remembered that he had used one to wipe up some ink he'd spilled and he guessed he'd better not find that one.

Mr. Carpenter finished reading the paper, drank his second cup of coffee, kissed Mrs. Carpenter goodbye and went off in his 1959 Chevy. Everybody relaxed when he left because sometimes Mrs. Carpenter would forget orders, but not Mr. Carpenter.

George was just having his third piece of French toast and was deciding whether he would have honey, maple syrup, or strawberry jam on it, when Awful Prentice came tearing down the street like a buffalo. You could see up the street for over a block from the porch and you could see Awful running all that way. His face was red and he was sweating so much that when he reached the Carpenter's he had to stop and wipe his face so that he could see. His crew cut looked like dry grass with dew on it.

He puffed for two or three minutes, standing outside the screened porch. When he got his breath he said, "George, you've got to come help me! My prayin' mantises—puff—puff—have hatched out. They're all over the house—puff—puff—and Mom says if I don't get 'em out in ten minutes she's going to take 'em up in the vacuum cleaner!"

George started to get up, taking his French toast with him, but his mother said, "Wait a minute, George. Your bicycle—those socks."

"Oh, yeah. Awful, I got to do some work first."

"But I can't wait!" wailed Awful. "Mom's going to take 'em up *now!* Think how you'd like to be sucked up into a terrible big dirty balloon thing—have all your legs and arms broken and be left to die—smothered probably and . . ."

Awful sounded as if he were going to cry. "Couldn't your mother leave them there just a little while—say twenty minutes?" asked Mrs. Carpenter.

"No ma'am," said Awful. "She's having the Book Club to lunch and she's got to get the house cleaned and take a bath and set the table. It won't take long and I'll help George do his work right afterwards. Can't he, please, Mrs. Carpenter?"

"Well, I suppose so," said George's mother, who really was a good sport. "But you march yourself right back here, George, as soon as you've caught those creatures, and find that sock!"

George hastily devoured his French toast, thinking that if he choked on it, it would be in a good cause— and without the strawberry jam, too, a real sacrifice— and the two boys hurried to Awful's house.

The mantises were in his bedroom and there must have been a million of them. They were about as big as big mosquitoes and they looked as if they were made out of amber glass. You wouldn't believe how much like a grown mantis a baby mantis can look. They have the same long necks and tiny mean-looking little heads and the same tricky arms drawn up ready to snatch some other unsuspecting insect.

They were all over the bed and the curtains, on the screens and on the mirror of his bureau.

"What are you going to put 'em in?" asked George.

"Nothing," said Awful pushing up the window screen. "I already have a few in my collection. We've got to get these outdoors. If they don't get something to eat soon, they'll die."

"What can they eat?" asked George. "Their mouths must be littler than the point of a needle."

"They eat other insects. There's lots of 'em born every year, but only some of 'em grow up."

"Maybe they eat each other," said George, staring at a cluster of the little glassy figures. "Perhaps that's why only some of 'em survive."

"None of these are gonna survive if Mom gets here," said Awful. He could hear the vacuum cleaner in the hall getting closer and closer.

"How do you get 'em out?" George asked, picking one up. It gave him a horrid, creepy feeling.

"Gosh, they sure are brittle," he said. "I didn't mean to kill it."

"A lot of 'em'll die anyway," said Awful sadly. "Lizards eat 'em, and birds and other insects. I guess that's why they have so many babies in an egg. There wouldn't be enough to go around otherwise. Look, most of 'em are going out by themselves."

They were too. As soon as the screen was raised the tiny insects had begun to spring out of the window. They poured over the sill like a waterfall with a purpose and a swiftness that was almost horrifying.

"Looks weird," said George in a hushed tone.

"It's instinct," said Awful. "Like those lemmings that go to the sea. They know they ought to be outdoors."

"Why do they know it?" asked George, staring at the tide of fast-moving insects, a lot of which were hopping up and down, leaping onto the bushes outside the window or sailing off like tiny parachutists. "The lemmings get drowned and the mantises get eaten up. It doesn't make sense to do something like that."

"I reckon it all works out—you know as they say— the law of nature, or the balance of nature. I guess lizards have to eat, and birds, too, and maybe something has to have the lemmings—something that lives in the ocean."

"Yeah," said George, "I can just hear some big old codfish saying, 'I must have a piece of lemming pie!'"

"Ugh!" said Awful. "Look, most of 'em are out. Let's shoo these off the bed and the curtains. We'll never get 'em all out. Last time I hatched one of these things I kept finding 'em for days on the picture frames and in my clothes. I even went to school with one in my hair!"

They chevied and shooed and worked to get the rest of the baby mantises out. Those on the bed were the hardest. They just clung to the tufted spread and wouldn't move.

"These sure don't know what's good for 'em," muttered George, picking one off his neck and carrying it carefully to the window. "Say, here's two coming back in!"

He picked up a magazine and waved them back into the air.

Mrs. Prentice cut off the vacuum cleaner and called, "I'll be in there in about two minutes, Orville. Now you see that you have those nasty bugs out of there when I do."

"We'll have to take this spread off and shake it out the window," said Awful.

They did, and it got rid of most of them, but some of the mantises did not seem to have any instinct because they kept hopping back into the room. They had a hop better than any jack rabbit. It looked almost as if they were flying.

Awful took five or six up in a glass jar. He dropped in some cotton with potassium cyanide on it and covered the jar.

"Gosh!" said George, horrified as the tiny mantises sat there unmoving and obviously dead.

"They haven't been alive long enough to know anything," Awful reassured him. "They probably think this is all there is to life."

This was a depressing thought and George was glad that just then Mrs. Prentice came in and started shoving things around so that she could vacuum the rug. She had a dust cloth and she made a swipe at the bureau. But there was a bottle of preserved snakes there and a cocoon and a few other things and she couldn't dust very well.

"Orville Prentice," she said, getting a little red in the face, "if you don't move all this mess out of your room,

I don't know what I'm going to do! And there's that dead frog I told you about last week. Get it right out of here—and now!"

"I don't see why that bothers you," said Awful, flipping a couple of mantises out into the shrubbery, "it doesn't smell and it's perfectly dry."

His mother looked at him and he said, "Oh, all right!" and picked the frog up by one leg.

Mrs. Prentice shuddered and started the vacuum cleaner. The noise must have scared what baby mantises there were left, for suddenly the room seemed full of them again, hopping and jumping in every direction. Mrs. Prentice screamed and started shoving the nozzle of the machine at them as if she were fighting a duel. Poor Awful looked as if he'd like to bawl so George said, "Well, the birds and lizards won't get them," to remind him something probably would have happened to them anyway.

Pretty soon the mantises all seemed to be gone, except maybe a few Mrs. Prentice would never notice. George and Awful went downstairs and out into the yard with the frog. Awful went next door and stuck it up against the window screen over Miss Mullin's sink and hoped he'd be there when she looked up from washing the dishes and saw it.

"I don't know why people have to be so fussy about their old houses," he said. "You can't have anything or your mother is all the time yackin' about it."

"My mother's the same way," said George. "And that reminds me I've got to go back and find my sock and things. Come on, you said you'd help me."

They got back to the Carpenter house in time to hear Karen wailing, "I don't *have* any more room on my closet shelf! But I've had my bears for years! I know I don't play much with them now, but I might want to sometime."

In between they could hear Mrs. Carpenter's voice. Although they couldn't make out the words, they had a good idea of what she was saying.

"See what I mean?" muttered Awful.

"You don't want me to have anything," bawled Karen, the way she did when she wanted to get her own way and acted pitiful.

"Now, Karen, you know that's not true." Mrs. Carpenter had come into Karen's room and they could understand her now. "It's just that this house is for all of us. Your father and I have a right to have our friends here without being embarrassed by its always looking like the city dump. You have a whole room to yourself and I let you do what you want to in it as much as possible. But you are too big to have stuff all over the floor and the tops of everything and under your bed— so much stuff that nobody can even get in here to clean. Now either find a place for these things or give them away. It's really wicked to have so much you don't need when other children have nothing."

George rolled his eyes at Awful and Awful drew one finger across his throat. Then they sneaked around to the front door. After they had moved the bicycle, they went up to George's room. There were a lot of old socks under the bed, a baseball George had been missing, a bunch of comics, a Hershey-bar wrapper, a sweat shirt, a copy of *Sam Sanders, Boy Sleuth* that belonged to Andy Medders, and the new sock.

"I better just throw this one away," George said holding out the sock with ink stains on it. It had been white, but it was now a blotchy blue. "It'd be better never to find it than to have her see this ink on it. I forgot it was one of the new ones."

"You can get the ink out if you soak it in buttermilk," said Awful.

"You can?" asked George, surprised.

"Sure. You got some?"

"I'll see."

George shoved the rest of the stuff back under the bed and carried all the socks downstairs. He put all but the inky one in the clothes hamper in the laundry room and then he went to the refrigerator. There was a carton of buttermilk there and he took it out. He opened the container and stuffed the sock into it.

Just then Mrs. Carpenter called out. "George! Is that you? Have you gotten that mess out of the living room?"

"Yes'm," said George, and put the buttermilk quickly

back into the refrigerator. He hurried across the hall and went into the living room, where he gathered up the pieces of his model airplane.

Awful was walking behind him and didn't see the glass of water that Karen had been using for her paints.

Of course he knocked it over. The rug was pale gray and the paint used was red with a lot of black near the bottom of the glass. It made a long puddle, shaped something like a frying pan, and then sank into the rug.

"Great jumping snakes!" muttered George. "That stupid kid—leaving a glass on the floor." He picked up the evening paper and began to wipe at the stain but it still looked terrible.

"Move the chair a little," said Awful. "Maybe it won't show."

"This is a practically new rug," said George. "She'll notice right off. If there had been only black in the water it wouldn't be so bad. We could wash it a little and maybe it would be gray."

"Let's try washing it anyway," said Awful.

They sneaked into the kitchen for a dish towel. George wet it at the sink and they scrubbed the stain. They couldn't tell whether the stain was all out or not because the wetness made a very dark spot. But as George said, there was nothing else to do but wait until it dried and hope that his mother didn't see it first.

They collected the parts of the model airplane and went out on the screened porch.

Karen was in her room, working hard at finding places to hide her treasures. She couldn't imagine why grownups fussed about keeping things under a bed. It was such a convenient place. Things were so handy there, and if you pulled the spread down nobody could see anything. It was amazing, too, how much you could get under a bed after you'd had a little practice. She found a piece of bubble gum she had stuck to the side of the bed two nights before and chewed on that while she worked.

She was out in the pantry, looking for some boxes in which to pack her bears and her old Raggedy Ann and Andy dolls when Mrs. Sissom arrived to do the laundry.

She came in and took off her little squashy black hat, which always reminded George of a burned popover. Mrs. Sissom usually had a cup of coffee when she got to the Carpenter house, but this was a hot morning and of course she would pick this day to have a glass of buttermilk.

She took the buttermilk out of the refrigerator and a glass from the china cabinet, and began to pour. Suddenly she gave a shriek like a tire squealing, and flung the carton across the kitchen.

"There's a *rat* in there!" she yelled. "Look at the nasty gray creature!"

The carton lay on the floor, and George's wet sock, which had now faded to a sickly gray and did look pretty ratty and horrid, was lying halfway out of it.

Karen, being silly like all girls, gave it one look and jumped up on the kitchen table, yelling at the top of her voice.

Mrs. Carpenter, Awful, and George came running. As soon as George saw the milk carton he groaned and sank onto a chair.

There was a lot of fuss and excitement while George tried to explain to his mother that he had only been removing the ink stains from his new sock and that he had thought she would appreciate it. How did he know, he pointed out reasonably, that Mrs. Sissom would drink buttermilk today? She usually had coffee.

"I'll never do it again in my whole life!" said Mrs. Sissom with unnecessary firmness. "I'll never pour out no kind of milk without seein' that nasty-looking creature!"

"Good grief!" cried George. "It's just a sock! You wash socks all the time."

"George!" said his mother.

It was a tone he knew he could not argue with. He went over and picked up the sock—which *was* pretty slimy and gruesome looking—and threw it in the sink. Then he got a sponge and cleaned up the mess, throwing the carton into the garbage pail.

"Let me fix you an iced coffee," said Mrs. Carpenter to Mrs. Sissom, who was so shaken that she had to sit down and fan herself with her hat. "Sometimes," went on George's mother, "I think children should have a separate house to live in."

"I knew a family like that," said Awful. "The man bought two houses and made a sort of hall between 'em, and the children hardly ever came over on the parents' side."

"Well, I don't know that that is a good idea, either," said Mrs. Carpenter. "It doesn't sound very happy. But I do often wish you children had some place to carry on all your different activities."

"What we need is a clubhouse," said Karen.

"Just what I was going to say," said George.

And that's how the whole thing started.

2 ꙮ After school the next day, which was Friday, George called a meeting. Awful was in on it, of course, and so was Shelby Fox who lived next door to George and raised all kinds of pets. Then Karen insisted on asking her best friend, Monica Raney, who brought along her little brother Owen who wasn't very bright.

Shelby's folks had a barn on their place so they met up there in the loft.

"Why wouldn't this make a good clubhouse?" asked Karen.

"Because my brother Bill uses it to practice in," said

Shelby. "See?" He pointed to an old recorder in one corner and a guitar leaning up against the wall. "Buzzy Morton comes over and plays his horn here too. His folks won't let him practice at home because his mother's nervous and he wakes the baby."

"It looks like nobody wants kids to do what they want at home," added Awful.

"Yeah," said Shelby. "My mother said almost all they talked about at the Book Club yesterday was the way children clutter up the place."

"I don't suppose they did when they were children," said Monica crossly.

"They had bigger places then," said George. "They had attics and big porches and everybody had barns. You hardly see any porches now and what attics people have are insulated or something so you can't play in 'em."

"It's what they call a social trend, I guess," said Awful, who liked people to think he knew everything.

"Well, whatever it is," said Karen, "we've got to do something about it. What we need, as mother said, is a whole house where we can keep our collections and stuff."

"And that's why we've got to have a clubhouse," declared George. "But I don't see how we'll ever get one big enough."

"We'd have to build one," said Shelby, "and you

know what that means. You can hardly ever get any old lumber nowadays. And there are all these old cruddy laws about building anything on your own property—zoning or something."

"And it would have to be bigger than we could possibly build if we're going to put all our things in it." Monica looked glum. "My collection of dolls, for instance, and Owen's hats and all our comic books."

Owen collected hats. He had a fireman's hat, a policeman's hat, a cowboy hat—all sorts of hats, even one he "got off" a tramp for a quarter. His mother made him keep that one on the back porch. He was wearing his mounted-police hat this morning.

"Yeah. And we ought to have some books in the clubhouse for rainy days," said Shelby. "I need room for my cages and boxes. I could have a lot more animals if I had some room. My Dad's all the time fussin' about the garage being full of my stuff and my mother says my rabbit hutches look awful back of her flower garden." Shelby screwed up his nose, which already turned up, until it looked like a mushroom.

"It seems like parents have formed an anti-children union," said Awful. "But look at all the antiques your mother collects, Shelby, and the books Mr. Carpenter has all over his bedroom and the hall and living room!"

"And that silly blue and red glass your mother has in those cases," put in Monica. "I guess if grownups do it it's collecting. If children do it, it's just a mess."

"Well, we've got to do something about it," said George. "Why don't we have a committee to look into it?"

"Look into what?" asked Owen. He wore glasses and sunburned easily. Mr. Carpenter said he looked like a pink owl.

"That's what committees always do," said George. "They look into things and then tell the rest of the club or the board, or whatever, what to do."

"Yeah—but what are *we* going to look into?" asked Owen.

"The situation, stupid," said George. "The committee will look around and see if there is a place we can use for a clubhouse."

"Who'll be the committee?" asked Awful.

"I will," said Monica. "I bet I could find a place."

"There have to be two or three," said George. "You can be one and I'll be one and somebody else—"

"Me," said Awful. "I can go all around looking because I'm always looking for bugs and frogs and things, anyway."

George said, "Is that all right with the rest of you? In fact, we can all look. But the committee will have to be really responsible for getting the clubhouse. O.K.?"

Everybody said, "O.K."

"Tomorrow's Saturday. That'll give us a lot of time to look," said Karen. "Monica and I can go around together."

"What are we looking for?" asked Owen.

"An old empty shack, or a place that's falling down that we could fix up," said Shelby.

"But it will have to be big enough for all of us," said George. "We'll meet here tomorrow afternoon about four and see if anybody has found anything. Shall we?"

They all agreed on that too, and disbanded.

Early the next morning, George got on his bike and rode to the end of town, where the houses were far apart. They were big, mostly, with all sorts of turrets and little windows up near the roof and big porches and old trees in the yard. The sort of houses people used to live in and children would still like to, thought George.

Some of the houses were occupied, though they looked pretty shabby. The paint was peeling and the grass needed cutting. There were chickens wandering around in some of the yards, and in almost every one were a couple of clotheslines with overalls and sheets and things hanging on them. Every now and then there'd be somebody—an old man perhaps—sitting on the porch with his hat pulled down over his eyes, smoking or sleeping, or some ragged little children playing under the trees.

But mostly it was hot and quiet and drowsy with all those big trees and the chickens pecking and clucking and crooning to themselves the way they do.

Finally George saw just what he wanted, a great big

empty house, just standing there. It had a tumble-down picket fence. The grass was high in the yard and cedar trees grew right up to the house so you could hardly see the windows.

George rode his bike in at the sagging gate and up the gravel walk that had leaves and sticks all over it. It looked as if nobody had been in the place for years and years and as he got up to the house he began to wish that he had brought Awful or Shelby with him. Not that he was a coward by any means, but he had noticed in the programs he had seen on television that the really smart characters were the ones who worked in pairs, because otherwise something might happen to a lone adventurer and nobody would know it for days.

As these thoughts crossed his mind, he paused and surveyed the house carefully.

Most of the windows were gone and the shutters, unpainted and broken, hung here and there by one hinge or had simply fallen off altogether and lay on the ground.

There was a big porch almost smothered by a creeping green vine and since it had a good many holes in it—the porch, that is—George wisely decided not to walk across it and into the house.

Instead, he walked around outside and tried to peer into the windows. But the ones in front were too high and it was not until he got around to the back that he could see in at all. He tried the back door. It was open and he walked in. The place smelled musty and dusty.

The kitchen was bare except for a dirty table and a kind of cabinet thing. He cracked open the door and looked into the next room, all empty and almost dark because of the cedars and shrubs covering the windows.

When George realized that there were several more great empty rooms on the first floor and that the big dark stairway that went up from the front hall led to heaven knew how many dark empty rooms upstairs, he decided that he should go back and get the others before he went farther. After all, it wouldn't be fair, he thought, to see it all by himself the first time. If this was to be their clubhouse, the other members would have to pass on it too. It sure looked as if nobody else wanted it.

He was tiptoeing back across the kitchen when he caught his foot on a torn piece of linoleum. He fell flat and a tin plate he had not noticed on top of the cabinet bounced down with a loud clatter and rolled across the floor.

George got up, somewhat shaken and feeling almost as if somebody had come out of the pantry and attacked him from behind. He brushed himself off and started on across the kitchen. Just at that moment he heard a strange shuffling sound in the rooms above him.

"Squirrels," George told himself hopefully, but he still thought he would leave the place as soon as possible. He went out the back door, closing it carefully behind him. For a minute he stood there trying to remember on which side of the house he had left his bike.

He remembered passing an old chicken coop on the north side so he started back that way. But just as he got to the corner of the house somebody emptied a pail of dirty water on him from an upstairs window. George jumped aside but he was drenched in the stuff which smelled like kerosene and soap and garbage. When he had wiped his eyes, he looked up from the bushes, in which he had sensibly taken refuge and saw the bucket being drawn back inside.

George's feelings were hurt. He felt that if the creature who had drenched him had not wanted him there, he could have said so in a much more polite way.

He slogged his way aroung the side of the house— even his tennis shoes were full of the nasty water—and found his bike.

He looked at the house and was considering going back to tell the creature in there what he thought of him when there was a terrific roar from one of the upstairs window. Something went zipping past George's head so close that he could feel the air moving.

He felt that he was really not wanted here, so he mounted his bicycle and buzzed off as quickly as he could. So quickly in fact that he went clear across the road and into a blackberry thicket before he could stop. He couldn't be sure, but he thought he heard a cackle of laughter from the old house.

3 When he got home, George found that his mother had gone to the supermarket. He slipped upstairs and took off his wet, smelly clothes and threw them in the clothes hamper. Mrs. Carpenter said later that she could not understand why his things had mildewed when it had been such a dry week. He took a quick shower, and put his shoes on the roof outside of his window to air. He was glad it had turned so warm because his mother would probably let him go barefoot anyway, and if he had put on his good school shoes she would have asked questions.

He was still a little shaken by his experience at the

old house. His dash into the blackberry bushes had left his legs scratched and sore. But when he had restored his strength and calm with a soda pop, a piece of chocolate cake, and a cold drumstick, he felt well enough to lie in the hammock and read the new copy of *Mad* magazine that had just come in the mail.

Karen was off somewhere, no doubt looking for a clubhouse, he thought, smiling. As if she would have any idea where to look! It was an extra good issue of *Mad* and it was nearly noon before he heard his mother drive up and blow the horn—a sign she wanted him to come and help carry in the groceries.

After lunch, of all times, his mother reminded him that he had promised to cut the grass in the back yard. George went out, though still pretty exhausted from his morning's ride, and from eating four hamburgers and another piece of cake, and started the power mower. The back yard wasn't very big, but what with resting now and then, and stopping for a Coke, it took him most of the afternoon to mow the grass.

Besides, there were three large ant hills in the yard. George had just read a book on how industrious, clean, courageous, and clever the ant was, and he almost felt as if he knew these ants personally. He had to cut very carefully all around the hills, and help a few laggard or over-tired ants out of the way. That alone took an awful lot of time.

Karen had come home and eaten, helped put the

groceries away, tidied up the kitchen, and then had gone out again. She hadn't said anything about the clubhouse and George thought she had probably forgotten about it. You couldn't expect girls to keep their minds on anything important.

Around four o'clock he ambled over to Shelby's barn. All the other club members were there, sitting outside the barn on buckets, a wheelbarrow, and a couple of old benches. Shelby's dog, Snoopy, was lying in the shade of the sycamore tree.

Owen was wearing his cowboy hat. It was too big for him and kept sliding over his glasses. He was hunched up in a wheelbarrow, figuring on a piece of paper with a red crayon. When George looked at him in a puzzled way, Monica explained, "He's figuring. Awful told him that thing about

> As I was going to Saint Ives
> I met a man with seven wives

and he's trying to figure out how many were going to Saint Ives."

George grinned. You could always keep Owen quiet by asking him a riddle. He could never get one right off but he'd work and work at it.

Shelby said, "It's too hot up in the loft so we're meeting down here."

"And I've found a clubhouse," cried Karen, looking as smug as a new laid egg.

"You don't know that you have," said Monica loudly. "You don't know that we can have it."

"I bet we can—"

"Hush up, will you?" roared George. "The meeting

will come to order and we'll have reports. We'll begin with Awful," he said, giving Karen a squelching look.

Awful looked a good deal like his name. He was hot and grimy and one eye was so red he looked as if he had pink eye.

"I didn't find anything. That is, anything we could use," he said. "I had to clean my room this morning, then eat lunch. Then I went back yonder in the woods behind the creek. I remembered an old shack out there. I was looking for a vireo's nest anyway. The shack was there all right, but somebody's using it. The door was locked and I went to look in the window. It was open and of course there aren't any screens in that old place. Anyway, the window where I was was sorta high. I stood up to look in and somebody poked a finger in my eye. It hurt like the dickens, and I went back to the creek and bathed it, but I couldn't see for a long time."

Monica thought that was very funny, but George, having had such a harrowing experience himself, could sympathize with him.

"Well, you can look some more tomorrow," he said, "if your eye's all right. You better do something about that."

"I went around and tried to get us a vacant store or warehouse," said Shelby. "You'd think people who aren't using 'em wouldn't mind us having one, but you never heard so many excuses: they didn't want a lot of kids messing the place up, we might set it on fire, a man was thinking of renting it, they didn't want to be responsible, we might get hurt. Every place I went, it was the same thing."

"What about you, George?" asked Monica.

"No luck. I found a house—just the thing—but somebody had beat us to it. They were living upstairs!"

He didn't tell them about the narrow escape he had had from the human monster. They would have been envious of such an adventure, he told himself, and besides he would have to tell them that he left in such a hurry that he nearly broke his neck.

Karen was having a fit, trying to get a word in, but Monica said quickly, "I have a place you can use if you want to—our basement."

Nobody said anything for a minute. Mrs. Raney's basement was big enough to hold a small circus, but it was as spic and span as a medical lab. George once heard his mother say that you could wipe off Mrs. Raney's furnace with a white kid glove and not get it dirty. He could just see her face if she came down there and saw bowls of salamanders, dried snakes and live ones, birds' nests and rag dolls, comic books, chemical sets, and Owen's hats, including the one from the tramp, all over the place. Especially on days when they tracked in mud or snow or one of Shelby's animals got out and tore up something.

"We'll keep it in mind," said George kindly. He had heard Mr. Knox, the school principal, say that when somebody like Mrs. "Cuckoo" Cranston made some silly suggestion.

Monica sat back looking very pleased with herself. After all, she was the only one so far who had suggested any sort of place.

Then Karen said, very slowly, "Could I speak now? Or don't you want to hear about the *per-fect* place I found?"

George graciously gave her the floor, which was really the bare place in front of the barn door.

"There's a house back of our house, off in the woods," said Karen in a low mysterious voice. "It's empty, but it's got furniture in it. There'd be chairs and things so we could sit down or take our lunch there and eat it, and nobody's living there."

"That's fine," said George sarcastically. "We can just move into it. I'm sure nobody would mind our just moving in."

"But nobody's in it now. You can tell that nobody's been in it for ages and ages. There used to be an old man lived there, but he's not there now. I guess he died."

"But a house has to belong to somebody," said Shelby. "When you die somebody else gets it. Suppose they came and we were there? I saw smoke coming from there in March—or maybe it was about Christmas."

"There is nobody living there *now*," said Karen stubbornly.

"Maybe it's in litigation or whatever they call it," said Monica. "You know like when somebody dies and leaves some property and the heirs all fight over it."

Karen, disappointed at all these objections, said, "Well, if nobody else's going to use it, why can't we? We're not going to hurt anything. I've heard Daddy say houses run down when people aren't in them. We'd be doing them, whoever they are, a favor. And it's so close, we could come and go any time," she said, running down like an old clock.

"They wouldn't let us," said Awful. "You know how they are."

Everybody knew who "they" were. The grownups!

"Then we can't tell 'em," said George. "After all, we're doing this because we don't want to bother them. When our mothers see how nice and clean their houses are without our junk, and when we're not underfoot all the time, they'll be willing, I bet."

"Yes," said Awful. "If they find out, we can tell 'em then. If we can tell 'em we did it because they were all the time fussing at us for having our things all over the house, then they won't be able to say much."

"Especially after we're already in the clubhouse," said Karen. George knew she was right. If you ask a parent if you can do something they will most of the time say no. But if you've already done it, and they see how harmless and reasonable it is, they'll agree.

"So we must be sworn to secrecy," he said. "Everybody must swear never to tell where the club is or what we do there. That is, of course, if it suits us—the house I mean."

They all agreed to that. When George told them to hold up their hands and swear not to reveal where the club was—wherever they decided that was to be—and what they were doing there, or suffer some terrible punishment, they all agreed. That is all but Owen who was still figuring. When George said, "Owen, do you swear to secrecy?" Owen looked up and, squinting through his glasses, replied, "Twenty-one. No twenty-two—lessee, there was the man and his—"

"Owen!" bellowed George. "Swear you will never reveal the secrets of this club!"

"Oh—sure," said Owen.

"Hold up your right hand," said George, "and solemnly swear."

"I do," said Owen, waving the red crayon. "Did you say the man had *seven* wives, Awful?"

George gave him a look and Shelby said, "Let's go look at the house right now."

And so the club members set out along the path back of the Foxes' barn and through the woods behind the Carpenters' house.

4 🌿   They had only to walk a little way before they came out in a clearing. There under some big trees, surrounded by bushes and high grass, was an old gray house. It had been painted, but now the paint was faded into the wood so you couldn't tell which was paint and which was just old planks. It had two stories and a big porch.

There was a narrow front yard that went down in a rangy, untidy way to an old road. Across the road were more woods. The road was grown over with clumps of grass and weeds and it didn't look as if anybody would be coming along to bother them.

"Why this is the old Spears place," said George. "Mr. Spears died some time ago. Maybe nobody else wants it."

"Neat!" said Awful. "Real neat!"

There was an old wooden swing on the porch, with two seats and a slatted platform that you could stand on and swing the whole business back and forth.

"Oh, Karen, look!" cried Monica, running up on the porch and getting into the swing. It had a few broken pieces and couldn't swing too well, but Shelby said he could fix it.

"Come on," said George, "Let's look inside." He went over and peered into a window.

"You don't have to do that," said Karen. "The door's not locked. The key's on the inside."

It was a big door with narrow windows on either side and a funny old bell pull right in the middle of the front panel. When it was turned it made a rusty, burring sound.

"Don't!" cried Owen. "Somebody might be in there."

"There isn't anybody in there," Karen insisted. "There hasn't been for ages. You can tell if you go in."

"But the bell might make somebody be there," said Owen. His eyes looked as big as biscuits behind his glasses.

"Silly!" said Monica. "You can't make people just *be* if they aren't."

Owen still looked worried. When George bravely opened the door and the club members had crowded inside, Owen kept looking back over his shoulder at the bright sunshine out in the yard, where Snoopy was sniffing around in the bushes. He took off his hat so that he could see better and held it tight in both hands.

The house was rather dim and so crowded with furniture and pictures and draperies that two or three people might be there and not be seen for several minutes.

They stood just inside the door and George called out, "Is anybody here?"

His voice didn't come out the way he meant it to. In fact it was plain squeaky, so he said, "Hruum. It's dusty in here. *Is anybody here?*"

There was not a sound in the house.

"I keep telling you," Karen said, "it's just an empty old house that nobody wants. I went all through the downstairs this morning."

Remembering his experience of the morning, George had to admit that she had courage even if she was a girl.

"Why didn't you go through the upstairs?" asked Monica.

"You'll see," said Karen mysteriously and started across the hall.

George stopped to look about him. The room was quite large and in the middle of the ceiling was a hanging lamp with a tortoise-shell-colored glass shade and glass pendants. The walls were covered with faded red paper and dozens of pictures, all in wide gold frames, all dusty and old-fashioned looking. There were a lot of tables and chairs with velvet covers and a great big sofa with the stuffing coming out. A rug covered almost the whole floor, and there were smaller rugs on top of it, all dark and pretty dusty. The windows were practically hidden by torn lace curtains and heavy red draperies.

Karen had gone over to the foot of the big staircase at the far end of the room. She was pointing up and the others were staring where she pointed. George walked over and looked too and what he saw was a great tall gate or grill at the head of the stairs that locked off the whole top floor. There was a heavy old padlock and chain on it.

"My grandmother had one like that in her old house," said Awful. "It's to keep burglars from going upstairs."

"Well, it kept me from going up there too," said Karen, "but we don't need the upstairs. Come and see."

They walked slowly through the house, staring. And there was plenty to look at. All the rooms were furnished in the fusty, crowded, fancy manner of a century before which they had only seen in movies.

There were, besides the living room and a square hall, a study or library with rows and rows of dark leather-bound books on the shelves around the room. Then there was a kitchen and a pantry.

When they got to the kitchen and pantry the girls had a fit. The windows were rather dirty, and everything in it, the stove, the sink, a metal coal bin, and the pots and pans were worn and rusty. There was a big kitchen table covered with oil cloth which had once been blue and white, but was now just a faint mixture of both, and there were some low cupboards along the walls with doors on them.

"Well, I must say this place needs a good going over," said Karen excitedly as Mrs. Sissom did when she came to the house after a party or something. "We'll bring mops and soap over and scrub brushes—say, I wonder if the water's on?"

"Of course not," said George. "People always turn off the water when they leave a . . ."

He said no more because Monica had moved over to the sink and the water was gushing out of the faucet. There was a dead roach in the sink, floating around on his back with his feet curled up. He looked real happy; the way you feel when you are floating out beyond the waves.

But Monica said, "Ugh!" and pretended to be sick.

"I wonder if that means they're coming back?" asked Shelby. "Maybe they left the water on because they've just gone on a trip."

"Are you crazy?" asked Awful. He had just been reading about Sherlock Holmes in *The Hound of the Baskervilles* and thought he would make a good detective. "Look how dusty everything is. Look at the road

outside. Look at that shed out there. The grass is high everywhere. There hasn't been a car here for years—if there ever was one. And all this rust—it'd take months for that to form."

"Maybe they just forgot it," said Owen.

"How about the lights?" Shelby reached up as he spoke and pulled the cord on a dingy bulb in the middle of the ceiling.

The fly-specked bulb came on, throwing a weak yellow light onto the shadowed room. A cheer went up from the onlookers.

"There's only one thing," said George. "How are we going to come over here all the time and keep this club a secret? I mean they'll be asking where we're going and where we've been. You can say 'Out' but sometimes they say 'Out where?' "

"That's easy," said Monica. "I'm over at Karen's. Karen's over at my house. You're over at Awful's and he's at Shelby's and—"

"And I'm at George's!" said Shelby with a whoop of laughter.

"But suppose my mother calls me at your house and I'm not there?" asked Karen.

"Well, we're hardly ever *in* the house," said Monica. "My mother will just say that we are out playing somewhere and she will give us the message when she sees us."

"I guess it will work—for a while anyway."

"And remember," said Awful, "we said if we had to tell them, they would probably be so glad we had all our stuff out of the house that they won't make us give it up."

"There are more rooms on the other side," said Karen. They all left the kitchen and went back through the house.

"When we've seen all the rooms," said George, "we can each select one. How many are there, down here, I wonder."

"Six—or is it seven, counting the pantry?" asked Karen.

"There are six of us," said George.

"Karen and I want the kitchen and pantry," said Monica firmly. "But we'll share the kitchen. You boys are always wanting water and a place to mix things. We'll use the pantry for our dolls and bear collection."

"If that isn't just like girls!" screamed Awful. "Us boys have to share a room, while you want two!"

"There are two of us," said Monica.

"Besides we said we'd share the kitchen," said Karen. "And I bet if there's any cooking done we girls will have to do it!"

"Let's see the other rooms before we have a fight," said George calmly. He hoped Monica would want one of them because he had already decided that the glassed-in pantry shelves would be ideal for his model airplanes.

Back of the living room was a bedroom, a bath, and a glassed-in porch that was really a hothouse. It opened off a dining room. The hothouse, or conservatory, had benches and tables with lots of flower pots and boxes full of dry dirt and withered plants. The sloping roof was made of glass that had been painted white.

"Hot dog!" yelled Shelby. "Just the place for my animals! Boy, is this neat or is this neat!"

"I'll take the dining room for my collection," said Awful, "then when any of your things die I can mount 'em right here."

Shelby was a little taken aback by this, but he didn't say anything for just then Karen shouted in a horrified voice, "Look! Look at that *thing* in the window!"

They all turned and then stared as if frozen. A face so horrible and sinister it made their flesh crawl was pressed against one of the dirty hothouse windows. Even George felt a shiver go through him and Monica buried her face in Karen's T-shirt and moaned.

They stood there for a minute paralyzed, and then the face moved back. A hand came up and knocked on the windowpane and a high squeaky voice said, "Lemme in. What're you guys doing in there?"

Everybody went limp with relief. It was just old Squeaky Morton with his nose flattened up against the glass, butting in as usual.

They opened the window and told him to come around to the front door.

There is a fat boy in every neighborhood and Sammy Morton was the one in this one. He was really fat and had a tight squeaky voice, but he could blow a trumpet like nobody's business and do an imitation of Louis Armstrong that was practically professional. Most people think that fat people aren't bright, but that's a mistake. Squeaky was a whiz at chemistry and he wasn't a dud at other things either. The trouble was that he was so fat he couldn't do a lot of things other boys did like racing and swimming long distances and such.

"We should have thought of Squeaky," said Shelby as they walked back to the living room. "He's always hanging around and he would've found out in no time."

"Yes, we'll have to ask him to be a member of the club," said Monica, "or he'll go blabbing it all over the place."

Just then Squeaky came bouncing in, wiping the sweat off his face.

"What're you doing in here?" he asked. "Ain't this somebody's house? One of you going to buy it?"

"Sit down," said George, "and we'll explain everything."

"How did you know where we were?" asked Awful, who thought they might have left some glaring clue that others would uncover.

"I was up in my room," said Squeaky, "with my binoculars and I saw you all take off behind Shelby's barn. I followed you and when I saw Snoopy lying out under that big tree in the back, I knew you were in here."

"Elementary," muttered Awful.

George then told Squeaky about the club and swore him to secrecy. Squeaky said he thought it was a keen idea and he would take the kitchen for his chemistry lab.

"You can't," said Monica. "We're going to clean it up and use it for all of us—to cook in and do anything we want."

"That's what I said," said Squeaky, grinning, "I want it for my lab."

"Say! Maybe there's a basement!" cried Karen. "There'd probably be a sink or washtubs or something down there."

"That'd be all right if there's enough light," said Squeaky.

"There are lights," said George. "But suppose something blew up. It would come right up through the whole house. It's too bad we can't get upstairs."

"Why can't we?" asked Squeaky.

They told him.

"Shucks, why don't you file the chain."

"No!" said George quickly. "That would be 'breaking and entering.' You know what that is, don't you?"

Squeaky looked impressed. "I reckon it would, at that. But what about down here?"

"We didn't break in. The door was open."

"Oh," said Squeaky.

"There was a door in the kitchen and I think it went to the cellar," said Karen.

They all went back to the kitchen and sure enough, when they opened the door, which stuck but wasn't locked, there were some rackety old stairs going down into a cobwebby, damp-smelling cellar.

"You'd better be careful on those stairs, Squeaky," said Shelby. "They don't look as if they'd hold more'n a couple of tons."

"Shuddup," said Squeaky, and started down. The stairs were all right and there were some windows in the cellar, but grass had grown up over them and there were spider webs and coal dust on the insides. There was, just as Karen had guessed, a sort of sink and some big tubs and a table at the other end of the cellar and a little stove with one lid on it, and a pipe that ran into the furnace chimney. The furnace was rusty like the stove upstairs and a rat jumped out when Squeaky went by it.

"You'll have company," said Awful.

"And the bubonic plague," said George.

"Hardee-hardee-har!" said Squeaky, trying the water faucet.

"I'll have to have a big light bulb," he said, "even if these windows are washed. But it'll do." He came back upstairs.

5 🌿   "I think we should have a meeting," said Monica.

"What for?" asked Shelby.

"To decide officially which rooms we'll have and then to decide how we'll get our stuff over here without all the grownups asking about what we're doing with it."

"That's going to be a problem, sure enough," said George.

"I think we can manage it," said Karen. "They've all been fussing about the mess and clutter so we could act as if we were going to do better and clean it up. We could make one big swoop of it, or move things a little at a time so they wouldn't notice. We could even leave a few things so that it would be cluttered just a little bit. Then they might not notice we'd moved the rest."

George looked at Karen in surprise and so did the other boys. It was almost frightening to think how girls could deceive people so easily.

"That'd be neat," said Awful.

"They won't like it," said Owen.

"They don't like the way it is now," said Karen. "I bet they'll think we are real good to get all that stuff out of the house."

Each member of the club had a sneaking idea that his parents wouldn't think it was very good to use somebody else's house without permission.

"That's what's called 'attenuating circumstances,'" said Awful, knowing full well what they were thinking.

"What's that?" asked Monica.

"Well, it means that if you do something wrong and you have a real good reason for doing it, they don't give you as big a penalty—I think."

"Like if you are shoved around too much and then you sock somebody. They figure it was his fault as much as yours," said George.

"And we were certainly shoved around about keeping our 'junk' in our homes," said Karen glumly.

"That's right," said several members of the club.

Then Monica said again, "We've got to have a meeting."

They all went back to the living room and sat around on the dusty chairs and the broken-down sofa.

"I will be the chairman," George said. "Somebody has to do it. First I think we should select our rooms and if there's any arguing we'll draw straws. I want the pantry."

"You can't have it," said Monica. "We need the shelves."

"But I need 'em myself," said George reasonably.

"There are shelves in the library," said Karen, "and a mantelpiece. You can take the books off the shelves and put your models on them and then you can put a really super one on the mantel."

"Yeah. I'm thinking of making a ship model next and it would look super on the mantel."

"And there's a table to work on there," said Monica firmly.

"We ought to put this all down," said George. "In writing, I mean. Anybody got a pencil?"

Owen still had his red crayon and the piece of paper he had been figuring on.

"You can write on the back of this," he said, "but I want it back. I haven't finished figuring out about Saint Ives."

"All right," said George, "we'll give the paper back to you. But you must tear it up as soon as you're through. This is a secret society and everything about it is confidential."

"Is it?" asked Owen.

"Of course it is, stupid! Didn't you promise not to reveal anything about this club?"

"Oh, sure!" cried Owen, looking relieved.

"Well then, you must keep everything we do a dark

secret," said George. "You can't go leaving information like this around for anybody to see."

"It would be a clue," said Awful, "a big clue to where we are and what we are doing."

Owen looked impressed. "I'll tear it up right away and figure on another piece as soon as I get one."

"All right," said George and Karen said, "I think the club should have a name."

"The Collectors' Club," said Shelby promptly, and they all agreed it was as good as any other.

"We ought to name the clubhouse too," said Shelby.

"I don't know what," said Monica. "It's a curious sort of clubhouse."

"That's it!" cried Squeaky, laughing. "The Curious Clubhouse."

They agreed on this, too, and then they chose their rooms. George wrote it all down with the red crayon. The paper was wrinkled from being in Owen's pocket and with the red crayon, which was warm and soft, Awful said it looked like some sinister message written in blood. But what it said was:

PANTRY	— Karen and Monica
STUDY OR LIBRARY	— George
DINING ROOM	— Awful
BEDROOM	— Owen
SUNPORCH OR HOTHOUSE	— Shelby
CELLAR	— Squeaky
KITCHEN AND LIVING ROOM	— All members

"Now the first thing we've got to do is clean the rooms up," said Monica, "and fix places to put our things."

"And remember," said George, "don't be bringing mops and things over here that your folks use every day. They'll miss 'em and start wondering."

"Maybe we better buy one or two things out of our allowances," suggested Karen.

But it turned out that she and Monica were the only ones who had any allowance money just then. Squeaky had bought some stuff to make a rocket, Shelby was paying on a microscope and George had spent his on his latest model. Awful said he wasn't getting an allowance for a while. His mother was keeping it to pay for cleaning a hall rug on which he had spilled axle grease.

"We can buy some washing powder or ammonia or something," said Karen, "and you boys can rustle up some mops and brooms."

"And you can jolly well help with the work," said Monica, who always liked to act as if she were the boss, "if we're going to buy the cleaning stuff."

"Nobody said we wouldn't," said George crossly. "We'll each clean our own places and all help with the kitchen and living room. We'll start tomorrow morning."

"Tomorrow's Sunday. We'll have to wait till afternoon," said Shelby.

"Yes," agreed George, "and that reminds me. No one of us is to come over here by himself—herself—or whatever. It's one thing for a bunch of us to go barging into an empty house, but we've all got sense enough to know no one kid—especially the girls—should go into an old vacant house alone."

"Seven times seven is—forty-five, forty-six, forty-seven—forty-nine!" yelled Owen who had been sitting over in the corner in a purple velvet armchair, counting on his fingers.

"Does he feel all right?" asked Squeaky, staring at Owen.

"He's working a riddle," explained Monica. Squeaky said, "Oh." They all knew about Owen and riddles.

"All right now," said George, "we'll meet here tomorrow right after lunch. And you fellas bring some brooms and mops—maybe there are some old ones in the basement or garage that wouldn't be missed for a while. I'll get some rags. Mrs. Sissom always has a big bag of them hanging on the basement stairs."

"Twenty-one!" cried Owen. "Look, seven wives, seven cats, seven kittens. Three times seven is twenty-one."

"No," said Awful sadly. "All of *them* weren't going to Saint Ives. The man that told the story—the riddle—*he* was the only one going to Saint Ives!"

"He was?" said Owen in surprise. He looked as if he couldn't believe it. Then he put his cowboy hat back on and picked up the paper he'd been scribbling on earlier. He threw it in the empty fireplace.

"Hey—destroy that!" cried George. "That's got our

names and the rooms on the back of it. Can't you remember that all this is a deep secret?"

"Who's gonna see it?" said Owen. "There's nobody here but us."

"You never know," answered George darkly. "Somebody might come in. And that reminds me," he went on, "we got to be sure to always lock that front door."

"Then we'll be pretty sure nobody can get in here when we're gone," said Squeaky. But he picked up the paper Owen had thrown away and tore it into little bits.

"Shall we lock up?" said Shelby as they left.

"Yeah," said Awful, "we'd better if we're going to bring our stuff in there. Who'll keep the key?"

"We'll hide it somewhere," said George, "in case the one who carries it can't be here, and the others want to get in. But where?"

They poked around and Shelby spotted the bird's nest snug in the thick honeysuckle vine at the end of the porch. "There," he said, pointing.

"Good!" said George. He stuck the key down in the nest, and they clattered off the porch, feeling that everything was secure.

6 ❧ The next week was about the busiest any of the club members could recall. There really was a lot of junk to sort out. For once they didn't mind work because they were doing it to have more fun later on. Besides everything being such a secret made it exciting.

Karen and Monica were quite clever, George had to admit. They announced to their parents that they were sorry they had been so messy and that they were going to clear out most of their stuff. This was really the truth as Monica pointed out.

Fortunately Mrs. Carpenter had gone into another tizzy about the mess so that it seemed quite natural for

Karen to say that she would do better. When Mrs. Raney heard about the fuss Mrs. Carpenter had made, she gave Monica a lecture and Monica said she was tired of most of her things anyway and would get rid of them that very day.

The girls went through all their junk and after sorting out a few things they really did not care for and leaving them neatly in their rooms, they loaded the rest into cardboard cartons and lugged them out to the trash cans. Of course they made a big point of letting everybody see them do it. Mrs. Sissom even helped Karen. Mrs. Raney watched Monica from the window where she was sitting sewing. The plan was to slip back when nobody was looking, take the boxes out of the trash and carry them over to the clubhouse.

As luck would have it, the trash man came early on Friday. Before they could get their things back, the boxes were riding off on the top of garbage and ashes and a lot of branches that somebody had pruned off their trees.

George and Karen had come out together. George was on his way to the clubhouse with two of his best airplane models, which he truthfully said he was going to show to Shelby and Awful. When they got to the alley back of the house, Karen let out a wail that sounded like two wildcats and a stuck pig.

"They're gone!" screamed Karen. "Mr. Flint's taken all my stuff! All my best stuff! My bears! My paints— my baby doll!"

"Quiet!" said George between his teeth. "You want to give the whole thing away?"

"No, I don't want to give it away!" yelled Karen. "But Mr. Flint—"

"I know, I know!" said George, setting down his models on the bench near the garage. "But if you don't stop that blubbering you'll give everything away. And I mean everything—see? I'll get my bike and try to catch him."

"I'll take your models over to the club," said Karen as George came out of the garage, wheeling his bike. "And if you catch Mr. Flint," she added gloomily, "you bring my things back."

"Two big boxes?" cried George.

"You can put one in your bike basket," said Karen, "and I'll tell Shelby to get his bike and follow you."

"O.K." said George. "You be careful with those models, hear?" He pedaled off as Karen, carrying his models, hurried through the woods toward the clubhouse.

On the way he met Monica who was in a swivet too, having made the same awful discovery about the missing boxes. She had her bike and said she'd go with him. She said Shelby had a flat tire, and anyway they didn't have time to wait for anyone.

They set out, expecting to catch up with Mr. Flint in no time. But everywhere they went, they saw empty overturned cans and no garbage truck.

"I wonder what got into him?" said Monica, puffing

as they went up the hill past the schoolhouse. "He's usually late and as slow as cold molasses."

"He would pick today to get a move on him," muttered George, hoping that Karen hadn't stumbled and fallen on his prize model.

"Where does he go from here?" asked Monica as they rested behind the school and looked out over the fields and the streets below.

"I think the last place he goes is the filling station on the edge of town. He goes out Maple and back on Pine and so on, and then he does the cross streets. Squeaky and I've ridden with him lots of times when Squeaky was tryin' to pick up some parts for his inventions. After he goes to that filling station he goes to the dump—"

"Well what are we waiting for?" yelped Monica, and started down the hill on her bike. The road was rough and rocky and two or three times George thought one of them would hit something and be shot over the handle bars. But they made it and pedaled as fast as they could on the highway to the filling station.

They could see Mr. Flint standing in front of the station drinking a soda pop. His truck was loaded high. They tore along and were almost in calling distance when Mr. Flint climbed up into the cab of the truck and started shifting gears.

They yelled and yelled as loud as they could, both being almost out of breath, but the truck rolled off.

"That cruddy old thing makes so much noise he'll never hear us!" groaned George.

"And there's not another stop till he gets way out to the dump," moaned Monica.

However luck was with the two heroic pursuers. About a half a mile beyond the filling station the truck slowed down.

"Let's see if we can catch him," cried George breathlessly, and made one final spurt although he was nearly exhausted. Monica, too, pumped gallantly along, her face so red it looked like a balloon.

They got close enough to call to Mr. Flint, who had gotten out and was looking at his tires. He waited for them to catch up with him. He stared at them and then said, "Goin' somers?"

They both tried to tell him what the matter was but Monica, who had a higher voice, being a girl, was so loud that George, being a gentleman, gave up.

"Them boxes and stuff from the Raneys' and the Carpenters' is way under all the brush and that there paper and cans from the fillin' station," said Mr. Flint. "Couldn't git to it now. Have to wait till I dump it."

"Dump it!" screeched Monica, "and have our things all mixed in with garbage and ashes and—"

"If we could go with you," George broke in, "maybe we could unload all those branches and those bunches of paper and get to the boxes—and then you could dump the rest."

Mr. Flint looked at the truck, then looked up the road toward the dump, then back at them and their bicycles.

"Won't hurt to try, I reckon," he said, "but it beats me why you kids'd put stuff out in the trash when you didn't want it carried off."

"It was because we—" said Monica, but George gave her a hard kick on the ankle.

"It was a mistake," he said, trying to glare at her and look pleasantly at Mr. Flint at the same time.

"Oh, well, better put your bikes on top o' them branches up there. You can ride with me," said Mr. Flint. "Good thing I thought I had a flat tire. Never woulda heard you and woulda dumped them boxes in that hole out yonder."

They all climbed into the front seat, having put the bikes on top of the load—which wasn't easy. Monica and Mr. Flint had to hand them up to George who laid them on the branches and saw that they wouldn't slide off.

Both the truck and Mr. Flint smelled of garbage and they were glad when it started rolling down the highway with the wind against them.

Presently they came to the big empty hollow that the town was dumping its trash in now and Mr. Flint backed up to it.

"Throw them branches off when you get your bikes

down," he said, "and see if you can spot them boxes. If not I'll have to dump 'em. Can't stay out here all day."

With that he slumped down in his seat, pulled his grimy old hat over his eyes, and apparently went to sleep.

It was hotter than blue blazes on top of the truck right out in the June sun. And they had no sooner stopped moving when gnats and flies and a few bees started buzzing around. George hauled off the top branches and waved them around to get rid of the insects, and Monica hauled off a few more. Some of them were tangled up, and they had to tug to get a bunch small enough to lift. The ashes had blown all over the other stuff and in a few minutes Monica and George looked as if they had been trying to get down a chimney.

The paper wasn't so bad except that the bundles were pretty big and they were both tired by that time. Under the papers were all sorts of horrid stuff like potato peelings, egg shells, carrot tops, and tin cans.

Monica gave a yell and said she thought she saw her dolls' feet sticking out. They dug away like beavers now that they were close to their goal. Presently the three boxes, smashed and damp and smelly but still full of treasure, came into view.

"We've found them! Mr. Flint, we've found them!"

cried Monica with surprising strength. They say women are the weaker sex but George was past making anything but a faint croak by this time.

"Well, git 'em out and I'll dump the rest," said Mr. Flint, coming to life like an old terrapin that had been sunning on a log.

A few minutes later, the truck was empty. Mr. Flint told them to put themselves, their bikes, and the boxes back into the dump truck and he'd take them to town.

Sitting beside him George could understand why Mr. Flint smelled like garbage. He smelled that way himself and he wondered if he could get rid of it before his mother noticed.

"Let us out at the corner of Maple and Dunn Streets, please," said Monica. George took his thoughts off his unpleasant fragrance long enough to realize that she had picked a good spot. It was out of sight of their own houses and not too far from a path that led through the woods near the old house. He just hoped to goodness nobody they knew came by and saw them getting out of the truck and looking, as he told Monica, "as if we'd been buried and dug up."

For the first time he thought of the club members waiting for him at the house. They couldn't get in because he had taken the key by mistake the day before and he knew that Karen was probably thinking his trip had been a failure. She should have known that George never failed, but then you can't count on girls.

"I'll bet they'll be glad to see us at the clubhouse," he said to Monica, but he never dreamed of the reception they would get.

When they wheeled their bicycles out of the woods and into the grassy road behind the old house, the other members were sitting on the porch looking pretty disgusted.

George and Monica walked into the yard and the others just stared at them.

"Why, it's George," cried Karen suddenly. She jumped and ran toward him, grabbing a box.

"And Monica!" said Shelby in a tone of wonder.

"Who in the name of great leapin' dinosaurs did you think it was?" yelled George. "Have you all gone crazy or somethin'?"

"You should see yourselves!" squealed Squeaky. "Your faces and your clothes are so dirty we couldn't tell who you were."

"Boy, are you gonna catch it!" said Awful, staring.

"And you smell worse than Mr. Flint," said Karen.

"Thank *you!*" said George, exasperated. "Thank you very much. I go out and race myself to death chasing that stinking old garbage truck to get your junk you were stupid enough to let be carried off and when I get back my friends act like they don't know me!"

"I knew you," said Owen from under his police hat. "I knew you because of the boxes. They said you'd gone to get 'em."

"And you call *him* dumb!" snarled George.

He was tired and hot and he even felt dirty, which was a strange feeling for George who never minded a little grime.

"I guess we really do look funny," said Monica and giggled. "But, Karen, you really ought to thank him, we had a simply ghastly time getting this stuff back."

"Let's go inside," said George wearily.

"Oh, George," cried Karen as he unlocked the door, "I do appreciate what you've done. I truly do. It was just that—well, you ought to see yourself!"

They had gotten inside now and George did see himself in the big round mirror that hung over the marble-topped table in the front hall. He stared, unable to believe that the chimney sweep with the black smudges all over his face, the ashes in his hair, and the sunburn on his nose was really George Carpenter.

Monica gave one look at herself and cried, "Great heavenly days! Lead me to a water faucet!"

Karen went with Monica to the bathroom and the boys took George out to the kitchen. There wasn't much to wash with, but Shelby had brought a cake of laundry soap and a can of scrubbing powder and with an old sponge and some newspapers they got the worst off George.

"But you don't smell much better," said Awful. "You better sneak in and take a shower before your mother sees you."

"Yeah. I guess it'll take a shampoo and everything to get me clean. Girls!" he added disgustedly. "Who else would think of putting their stuff out to be carried off and then wanting it back."

"We didn't put it out to be carried off," said Karen, who had come in from the bathroom. "We—"

"I know, skip it," said George throwing himself into a chair. He really was pooped.

"Boy, what I wouldn't give for a cold Coke!" he groaned.

"I've got lemonade in a thermos," said Squeaky, waddling over to get the big jug he had brought in with him.

"You have just saved a human life!" cried George. "What do we drink it out of?"

"There are some glasses in the pantry," said Karen. "I'll get a couple and wash them."

Monica came in looking somewhat better, but rather as if she were mildewed all over. Karen had given her some cologne from a little sample bottle she had and Monica at least smelled a lot better.

She too fell into a chair and for the next few minutes the other club members sat about spellbound while she and George told of their race with the garbage truck and the heroic rescue of the girls' treasures.

Karen brought the glasses and they all took turns— George and Monica first because they needed it more— drinking the wonderfully cold sweet lemonade.

"Good old Squeaky!" said George as he drained his glass. "That was downright smart of you, pal!"

Squeaky beamed.

"Well, I guess we ought to start putting our things away," said Monica. "I feel as if I'd done a day's work already."

"There's not much left to do in the pantry," said Karen. "Just move those few dishes off the shelves. We can put them in the kitchen somewhere and wipe—"

"Hey!" shouted George suddenly sitting up and staring at the wall. "Look at that! Who did that? It wasn't that way when we left here yesterday!"

They looked in the direction in which he was staring. Over the mantel hung a large picture of a surly-looking gentleman in a tall hat. They had hardly noticed it before but now they really paid it attention. For somebody, somebody who must have gotten into the house after they had been there, had turned the picture upside down!

7 ❧ "Maybe there's a safe behind it," said Awful. "Maybe somebody was taking something out of it and we scared 'em off before they got it back straight."

"But that means they're in here now!" shrieked Karen. Owen rushed to the red draperies at one window and hid behind them. A cloud of dust blew out into the room. Karen went over to George who stood up and said bravely, "Well, if we scared them off that means they're scared of us. So we don't have much to be afraid of—I reckon."

"But how did they get in—or out?" asked Shelby.

"I want to go home," Karen wailed.

All this time Squeaky had said nothing, just stared at the picture. Now he said, "Why don't one of you fellers climb up there and see if there is a safe? If there isn't then we didn't scare anybody off, they weren't after anything and they aren't in here at all."

"What do you think did that, then?" asked George. "Mice?"

Shelby had gotten a chair and after putting a large book from one of the tables on it he could reach the picture. He touched the frame and then drew his hand back.

"Suppose it's a trap?" he asked, looking back over his shoulder.

"Oh, yes, don't touch it!" cried Karen.

"Here," said Squeaky, handing him a broom, "lift it with that and look behind it."

Shelby leaned as far back from the picture as he could, without falling off the chair, and very cautiously lifted one corner of the frame. The picture which was hanging at an angle slipped and settled again exactly upside down. It startled them so that the girls screamed weakly and Shelby all but fell over the back of the chair.

But when nothing happened, he tried again. This time after a little struggle, because the broom handle was round and slippery, he lifted the picture away from the wall.

They waited, breathlessly, and in a second Shelby let it fall.

"Nothin' back there but cobwebs," he said.

"It must just have slipped by itself," said Monica. "Maybe a truck going by on the highway or something like that started it slipping."

The rest said they agreed with her, but the incident had left them all feeling a little creepy. Everything in the room seemed a little strange and perhaps to be hiding something frightening.

"Let's put it back up," said Monica. "I can't bear the way he looks at us—as if he were mad because we're leaving him upside down."

"We can't reach him well enough," said Shelby. "I could just reach the bottom of the frame."

"There's a ladder in the cellar," said Squeaky, "but one o' you fellas will have to go down there with me. I mean I can't carry it by myself," he added.

He needn't have worried. They were all going with him. No one was going to stay alone in that big room or go into any of the others by himself. Maybe that portrait had turned over by itself, but the wire that held it must have been old and rusty. If it had done anything it would just have broken. It never would have slipped. Even if the nail had slipped it would have come on out when Shelby moved the picture.

George thought of all this and he was sure the others were thinking it too.

Owen had crept out from the dusty curtains, and

they all trooped out to the kitchen, bumping against each other and stepping on each other's heels.

Monica began to giggle nervously.

"What's funny?" asked Awful.

"It reminds me of that poem we had to learn last month," she said. "You know—*Horatius at the Bridge:* 'Those behind cried "Forward!" And those before cried "Back!" ' "

Then they clattered down the cellar stairs after Squeaky and back up again as he and George lugged the old paint-stained stepladder behind them.

A little later they had the portrait back in place. The bearded gentleman glared at them still, but at least he looked more comfortable.

"I feel better about him," said Monica. "Now he can't blame us for leaving him head over heels."

"He hasn't got any heels," said Owen. "He just goes to the waist."

"He probably has hooves and a forked tail," said Karen, frowning at him.

"Hush!" said Monica, in a low tone. "I feel as if he could hear us."

"Baloney!" said Shelby rudely. "Come on, let's get things put away."

"I couldn't bring much," said Awful, as they began to sort out the various boxes, cages, and pails they had brought. "Just as I was about to get my stuff together Mom found out about the vacuum cleaner."

"What about it?" asked Karen.

"Aw, I spilled some sugar in the kitchen last night," said Awful, "and I took it up with the vacuum cleaner. But this morning it was full of little old red ants and she had a fit."

The girls laughed and Squeaky said, "When I went to kindergarten, I spilled a whole bloomin' box of glass beads while Miss Webster was out to lunch. When she came back she sent me to the broom closet to get that old vacuum cleaner and she made me take 'em all up. But when she emptied the bag to get 'em out they were ground up almost to a powder. Boy, was she mad! But, gosh, she made me do it. It was all she deserved for having an old grinding-up vacuum cleaner like that!"

When Awful had arranged his jars of pickled rattle-snakes on the chest of drawers in the dining room, he helped Karen and Monica clean the kitchen. They sloshed buckets of water over the floor and as Awful was barefooted they gave him the stubby old broom and the washing powder and let him scrub all over the place. They washed and wiped the shelves and the dingy oil cloth on the kitchen table. Monica said they would have to bring some polish for the stove later.

Shelby arranged his cages of white mice and his tub with turtles along the benches in the conservatory. Owen was happy hammering nails to hang his hats on. There was a large, very dead spider on the window sill in the kitchen and Awful asked for it for his collection.

George wasn't making much progress in the library. The books on the shelves were big dull old ones, dusty as all get out, and no good as far as he could see. They had titles like *Home and Fireside Compendium*, whatever that meant, and *Farm and Poultry Care and Feeding*, *Harper's Magazine 1888 to 1889*, *Viola Amanda, The Story of a Gentlewoman*. They were all thick and heavy with brown and gold bindings and dreadful black and white pictures of hard-faced men and women, a few cows and pigs and some old stone buildings. By the time George had cleared two long shelves and had lugged the books out to the hall he was exhausted.

Squeaky was banging away down in the cellar, moving old boxes and sloshing water around.

"It's going to be neat down here when I get through," he called upstairs once or twice. "But I sure need a bigger light bulb."

All of a sudden Monica looked at her Mickey Mouse watch and said, "Great jumpin' rattlesnakes! It's twelve o'clock, and I'm not half through!"

"Oh, great!" yelled George from the library. "And I've got to sneak in and take a shower before lunch."

"We can come back this afternoon," said Awful. "I can get more of my stuff out then."

'I can't," said Karen. "I've got to take my music lesson. I wonder if this old piano is any good. Maybe I could do some of my practicing over here."

"Well, you haven't time to see now," said George. "We've got to beat it."

"Let's bring our lunch tomorrow," said Monica, "and stay all day."

"Yeah," said Squeaky who had come upstairs looking hot and dirty. "Let's bring some games, like Scrabble and stuff. Then we can stay and play—like a real grownups' club. You know like they play bridge and stuff."

They hurried out, all talking at once. George locked the door behind them and put the key in the bird's nest. Old Snoopy got up from where he was sleeping under a big oak tree and they pushed off through the woods all unaware that from an upstairs window two sharp eyes were watching them closely.

8 🌿 George barely got home in time to take a shower before lunch. If his mother hadn't been out in the yard, planting Shasta daisies in the front flower beds, he never could have gotten upstairs unnoticed and unsmelled, or been able to run the shower without her knowing it. It wasn't that Mrs. Carpenter would mind his taking a shower, but she would naturally want to know why. That would lead to his telling about the garbage truck episode—and that would lead to the girls' dumb stunt of putting their collections out in the trash—and the first thing he knew she would have wormed the secret of the clubhouse out of him and the whole fine plan would fall through.

He flung off his clothes, which sent up a little *pfff!* of ashes as they hit the floor, and hopped into the shower. He couldn't even wait for the water to run warm. It had just about gotten comfortable when he felt he'd better hurry out. His hair was wet and when he dried it the towel was black and dark gray all over. George dropped the towel behind the clothes hamper, hoping Mrs. Sissom would think the dirt came from dust on the floor. He slicked down his damp hair and shook his clothes over the clothes hamper, because if he put on clean ones his mother was sure to notice it. George guessed she'd just think he'd wet his hair to brush it and probably say something about how glad she was that he had begun to take an interest in his appearance.

But Mrs. Carpenter was in a hurry to get back to her gardening. Just about the time the meal started Mrs. Hutchins, who was president of the Garden Club, called her and Mrs. Carpenter carried her salad and cup of coffee to the phone and talked till George and Karen were through lunch.

Awful's mother had some friends in for bridge so he managed to sneak out a lot of jars with worms and caterpillars and insects in alcohol, and two stuffed owls. Squeaky brought over some tools and chemicals and some Hershey bars in case they got hungry before they had to leave. Shelby made a new cage in the hothouse for his favorite garter snake, whose name was Raymond, after Mr. Ditmars, the famous naturalist.

"Raymond sure will like this place!" Shelby said as he tacked screen wire over the top of the table. "It's deep enough so I could take out part of the dirt and leave him some space to play around in and still have enough dirt so he can burrow in it when he wants to. He can hibernate right here too. He's really going to think this is a super motel!"

He stopped to feed Lizzie the lizard a little marmalade, which Lizzie licked off his finger with a quick black tongue.

"I'm just going to leave her loose," he said to George. "She is used to living under the back steps and she comes when I whistle, so I think she'll stay around here. She could get out through some crack maybe, but I'll keep her with me as much as I can till she gets used to it."

Lizzie, who had run up to sit on Shelby's shoulder, was licking her chops happily and looking about the hothouse as if she liked it. You could almost see her grinning as she stared at the two flies buzzing against the dusty glass panes.

"This oughta be a good place to raise praying mantises," said Awful, sticking his head in at the door.

"Too many spiders," said Shelby.

"Wouldn't the mantises eat the spiders?" asked Awful in surprise.

"Not if they were to get messed up in the webs. They'd get their necks and those little claws wound up in the web and then Ol' Miss Spider would wrap 'em up and put 'em in cold storage."

"But I thought the mantis would just reach out and grab a spider like it does a fly."

Shelby shook his head. "Spiders have more sense. They just sit in their webs and wait for the dumb old flies and mantises and things to get all wound up in them."

"Well, I'll be darned!" said Awful. "I guess that thing about the spider and the fly wasn't all just poetry, huh?"

Shelby grinned. "I reckon so," he said.

Owen had arranged all his hats so he trotted around and helped the others, fetching nails and things for Shelby and helping George move more of the books. When Owen got tired of working he built a house of books in the front hall, big enough to get into. He got his coonskin cap and sat in there with the broom for a gun and fought off Indians all the rest of the afternoon.

George had the most work to do because he had to clear off all the shelves before he could arrange his airplanes. Awful came in to help him, but right off he found a book written about a hundred years ago, telling of the crazy ideas people had then about the world and about plants and animals. It was about sea serpents and about how sheep grew on trees and you could cut the wool off, like pruning a bush. They thought the world was flat and that Indians had horns. It was wild. Awful just sat on the floor and snuffled and snorted and kept saying, "Good night! Look at this crummy guy!" and things like that until Shelby came in and sat down beside him. Not only didn't they do any work, but George had to step over them all the time.

He had four long shelves cleaned and wiped off and most of his models in place when Squeaky came upstairs.

"Gosh, it's gonna take me a month to get all the dirt and stuff out of that cellar," he said, puffing as usual. "It's all sooty and damp and there's rags down there that have actually grown to the floor! I'm gonna need a shovel to get the floor cleaned off."

"I thought I saw one behind the cellar stairs," said Shelby. "I'll come down in a minute and help you."

"I got to rest a while," said Squeaky. "I got to have some quick energy," he added, pulling several Hershey bars out of his back pocket. They were bent a little, but the others seemed glad to share them.

"There's one apiece," said Squeaky, handing them out. "Here—I'll take that one—it's sort of squashed in the middle. You know this is what the mountain climbers eat when they get exhausted climbing mountains. It picks you up quicker'n anything."

"Does the flavor of sulphur add to it?" asked George,

making a face. "You shouldn't have carried them in the pocket of those old jeans. They taste of chemicals!"

"That don't make any difference to the nourishment," said Squeaky. "Anyway, be glad to get 'em. Suppose you were lost on a mountain and cold and hungry and they were all you had. And you don't have to eat 'em, you know. You can give 'em back."

George saw that Squeaky's feelings were hurt so he said, "I was just kidding. It was good you thought to bring 'em. You can hardly taste the sulphur if you hold your breath."

Squeaky looked real happy after that and they sat around on the old dusty furniture and chomped on the chocolate.

"I've got to go home soon," said Awful. "I've got some fossils comin' in the mail. Besides we've got company coming for supper and I promised Mom I'd take a bath. I wish we could live here all the time and stay dirty and not have to sit around when dumb old company comes and have 'em say, 'My, how this boy has grown! Do you like school? What year are you in?' and all those dumb questions they ask you."

"Yeah," said George, "you'd think they'd remember how they felt when they were kids, but they don't. Every single one of 'em says the same thing, 'My how you've grown! Do you like school?' You can't help growing and nobody but a sure enough stupid would *like* school!"

"Oh, I don't know," said Shelby. "I kind of like school."

"You're a nut," said George.

Just then Owen, who had finished his Hershey bar, raised the broom and fired at the portrait hanging over the mantel.

"Bang!" he said. "You're an enemy! Bang! Bang!"

Maybe his voice was so loud it shook something, or maybe the old picture was ready to come down anyway, but just as Owen said "Bang!" for the last time, the picture slid down the wall. It hit the mantel and bounced to the floor with a crash that made them all jump.

"What in tarnation did you want to do that for?" yelled George.

"Yeah!" wheezed Squeaky, "I swallowed an almond backwards and I'm probably gonna die!" He rushed out to the kitchen and they could hear him running water at the sink.

George and Shelby went over and picked up the portrait. It was almost as high as they were tall and when you saw it up close it was scarier than ever. The man's face was reddish and had knobs of paint on the cheek bones. His eyes looked alive and were as black as bits of coal. He looked as if he could really sneer at you.

"He looks like a vampire," said Awful.

"You're crazy," said Owen. "A vampire is a bat."

"You mean you never heard of Dracula?" asked George.

"No," said Owen, "but I know that's a man in that picture so he can't be a bat."

"Pay no attention to him," said Awful. "He's too young to know about such things. Where'll we put this thing anyway? The wire's broken."

"Let's stick it in that closet in the hall," said George, "and then we better go home. We can bring a picnic lunch tomorrow and spend the day."

"I'm going to bring my transistor radio," said Shelby.

"My record player," wheezed Squeaky hoarsely.

"Yeah," said George, "with some books and stuff we'll soon have it a real super clubhouse."

"Neat," agreed Awful.

They went all around the house and saw that the doors and windows were locked. The kitchen door to the outside had a bolt on it.

"If anything else is goofy when we get back tomorrow, we'll know it's an inside job," George said.

"Or a poltergeist," said Shelby.

"What's a—what you said?" asked Owen, looking scared.

"It's a kind o' ghost, only all it does is throw things or move things or break dishes or something."

"Just like Awful," said George. "How do you get rid of 'em?"

"Oh you have to pray over 'em or something," said Shelby. "I read about it in a book."

"Well, I hope we don't have one in this house," said Squeaky. "I don't want any of my jars or tubes or things busted."

"Or my butterfly cases or bottles of stuff," said Awful, looking glum.

"Don't be silly," said George. "It's all just made up, like a ghost story."

"No it isn't," said Shelby. "There was a big piece in one of the papers, with pictures of the people and the houses that poltergeists had been in."

"Do they do anything to hats?" asked Owen fearfully.

"They don't do anything to anything," said George crossly. "It's just a lot of stuff that writers think up every now and then when they run out of something exciting to write about. Come on, you all, I've got to get home."

Awful and George lugged the big portrait out into the hall and set it up at the back of the empty closet. Awful went out and as George was shutting the closet door he gave the picture one more look. The man seemed to stare at them as if he were alive and wanted to put an evil curse on them. George closed the door hastily, but the memory of that baleful stare followed him all the rest of the day.

They clattered across the porch and through the weedy yard and disappeared into the woods. Again the eyes that had watched them before, followed them until they were hidden by the trees and undergrowth.

9 ❧ Things went along fine at the Curious Clubhouse for several days. The day after the portrait fell, the club members brought a picnic lunch and stayed all day. Those who still had cleaning and arranging to do did them. Karen and Monica played with bears who took trips, had accidents, were rushed to hospitals and suffered horribly with moans and groans that annoyed the other members.

Owen, who had had less arranging to do than the others curled up on the dusty mattress in his bedroom and, wearing his motorman's hat, read comic books and ate peanuts. It was a simply wonderful day for Owen.

"You know," said Monica, while they were sitting around the living-room table eating the peanut butter and jelly sandwiches, the hard boiled eggs, bananas, oatmeal cookies, hot dogs, and soda pop they had brought, "it seems funny the grownups haven't noticed that we're gone so much, or that so much of our stuff is out of the house."

"Well, it's like you said," mumbled Squeaky with his mouth full, "they think we're with each other—which we are."

"And as for the stuff," said George, "we told them we'd get rid of some of it. It's like a pebble in your shoe," he added, "once you're rid of it you don't think of it."

The others looked at him with respect after this remark, but he modestly tried not to notice that.

"It can't last," said Awful glumly. "Something will happen and they'll find out. Owen or somebody'll spill it—and then we'll have to give this place up."

A gloom fell upon the company. They looked around at the heavy draperies, the dusty furniture, the dark broad-framed pictures, and the fancy vases and whatnots that had already become dear to them. They might have become quite miserable if Owen, whose mouth had been stuck up with peanut butter, hadn't gasped and said, "I will not so too tell! I swored to keep a secret!"

"I don't believe he will," said Monica. She handed

him his bottle of orange pop because he was getting red in the face trying to swallow the blob of dry peanut butter.

"No, you and Karen, putting your junk out for the trash came nearer doing it," said Shelby. "What a nutty idea that was."

"It was not!" yelled Karen. "It wasn't our fault that old Mr. Flint came extra early. If one of your crazy animals doesn't get out and scare somebody, or Squeaky doesn't blow us up—we'll be lucky."

George could see that this would lead to a useless wrangle so he got up from the table and said, "I've got to get back to work. I got a book from *Popular Mechanics* about designing your own planes—not making 'em from kits—it's neat. Come on, you guys, I'll show you."

The girls knew that "you guys" did not include them.

They gathered up the paper from the sandwiches and carried the bottles out to the kitchen. Karen and Monica started acting out a soap-opera mystery with their dolls and a couple of toy soldiers that had been Owen's.

George on his way to the kitchen for some water overheard them talking.

"I'm sure glad they started making more boy dolls," said Karen, looking at the toy soldiers with dissatisfaction. "This black-haired one is the murderer."

"I'm going to have this blond for the detective," said Monica.

Squeaky and Awful went down to the cellar to work on an experiment and Shelby stayed to watch George work on his plane. Owen crawled back up on the bed and read his comics until he went to sleep.

Outside the summer breeze stirred the leaves in the thick woods around the house. From the library windows George could see Snoopy sleeping under Shelby's rabbit hutches in the yard. Two squirrels came down and squeaked and chattered at him, but he only twitched an ear and slept on. It was as peaceful as a little island in a tropical sea.

Sunday the members did not go to the club. When they went over on Monday they discovered that somebody had let all of Shelby's animals out.

"You didn't come over here yesterday did you?" George asked him as they stood in the doorway of the hothouse and stared at the empty cages.

Shelby shook his head. "I left enough food and water for two days," he said. "I can't understand how all of 'em could have gotten out. If I had a monkey or a raccoon I'd know one of them had done it—but snakes and lizards and crickets—not even the white mice could do this! I guess I was right—there has to be a poltergeist in here. The place was locked up tight."

"There's got to be some other explanation," said George. "We all know there's no such thing as ghosts."

"Old Miss Diggins saw a ghost," said Karen, who looked as if she'd just seen one herself.

"No, she didn't," said Monica quickly. "She just thought she did."

"She did too!" cried Karen. "It was a tall man dressed all in black. He passed her right in front of her house under the street light and took his hat off to her. She said you could see right through him."

"I wish you'd hush!" groaned Squeaky. "You give me the jitters."

"I got to get all my animals back in their cages—if I can find 'em," said Shelby.

"We'll help," said Awful.

"Be careful!" Shelby grabbed him by the arm. "You might step on some of 'em. It's hard to see 'em under these seed frames or whatever they are."

The frames ran all around the room under the windows. Down the middle of the room was a narrow flower bed that had once had tall plants growing in it, but they were all dead now. Shelby said it would make a great spider hotel after he got a cage for Lizzie. He'd found he couldn't leave her out as she ate all his insects. Of course Lizzie was out now and so were the mice and the three crickets. Awful located Lizzie on the window sill behind some watering cans. There were legs and tiny bits of cricket all around her so it was plain where the crickets had gone.

One of the white mice was in an old glove on a tool box in the corner and one went back into its cage while they were looking for the others. The third one couldn't be found and neither could Raymond.

Old Cooter, the terrapin, that Shelby had turned loose in the long flower bed, was there all right and

Squeaky said he might have eaten the third mouse. But Shelby said Raymond would more likely have eaten the mouse. Cooter was a vegetarian he said. Shelby had decided to plant a garden in that bed in just a few days so that Cooter could do his own rooting and eating. The

spiders could climb around anywhere they wanted to.

"Old man Cooter is a champeen rooter!" yelled Awful, who could be pretty silly at times.

"Raymond could be in among those plants," said Shelby. "What about you fellers helping me clean this bed out now. We can pull up those old plants and dig it up real good and I can plant seeds in it tomorrow."

"Will you plant some lettuce and radishes so we can eat some too?" asked Monica.

"Sure—if Cooter doesn't beat you to 'em. And I'll plant some beets too," he added, laughing. "That's where I found Cooter, nosing up Dad's best beets and chomping on 'em."

They spent most of the morning pulling up the dead plants. The dirt was so dry they came up easily. They didn't find Raymond, even when Shelby got a spade and dug up the soft earth. The job took quite a little while as the dirt spilled all over the floor and had to be swept up. Then Awful kept stopping them to look for stones for his rock collection, and John Silver, Shelby's one-legged catbird, kept hopping around looking for worms.

"If we could find some dry worms we could invent instant worms," said Awful, who was down on his knees grubbing for stones. "You know—just soak 'em till they puffed up again."

George said this was a revolting idea and hit Awful with the broom.

They didn't find Raymond for two days. When they did, he was lying along the wooden rail that ran around the top of the room watching them as if he enjoyed seeing them look for him.

It was on Wednesday that George had the shock of his life. It all happened because Mrs. Sissom ran out of washing powder and had to have some right away because the clothes were already in the washing machine. Mrs. Carpenter had gone into the city with her husband as she had an early dentist's appointment, so George had to go over to Meany's Little Supermarket and get the stuff. He was just coming out with the package, drinking a bottle of pop to pep himself up for the day's work, when he almost ran smack into this man.

In a very small town everybody knows everybody else. A stranger is something to notice and the sight of this stranger made George's hair grow about two inches in as many seconds. The man was thin and dark, he had a black beard, high cheek bones with red spots on them, and mean, dark, deep-set little eyes. In other words, he was the man in the portrait at the clubhouse!

He glared at George so hard that the bottle of pop slipped out of George's shaking hand and broke with a loud *splop!* and a crash on the sidewalk. A piece of glass cut George on the shin, but he didn't even know it until later because he was so astonished and shocked at meeting this gruesome character face to face.

The man gave George a positively withering look and brushed past him as he went into Meek's Drugstore. George hurried home with the washing powder and tossed it onto the kitchen table.

He was just going out the door when Mrs. Sissom screeched, "What on earth have you done to your leg? Look! You're bleedin' all over the linolerum." Mrs. Sissom often got the names of things wrong. George looked down, and sure enough, there was drops of blood on the kitchen floor from a most dramatic, slow stream of blood on his shin.

"Musta scratched it," he muttered, and grabbed a cloth off a chair.

"Not that!" yelled Mrs. Sissom. "That's a dish towel. Here." She handed him a bath towel and then went to get the first-aid box Mrs. Carpenter kept in the pantry. She washed the cut, muttering that it was the deepest "scratch" she'd ever seen, and dabbed some iodine on it.

"Ye-ow!" screamed George. "Did you hafta do that? Lemme go! It's all right! I got some important things on my mind. Leggo my foot."

"Just you hush," said Mrs. Sissom, panting a little from hanging on to George's ankle with one hand and trying to put a band-aid on his leg with the other. "Want to go outer here lookin' like a stuck pig? And now I got this floor to wash before I'm through with the clothes."

George thought this was an ungrateful remark after he had gotten wounded while fetching the washing powder. He thanked her for fixing his leg and limped off as fast as he could to the clubhouse.

He stood in the middle of the living room and yelled and the club members came out of their rooms like fiddler crabs out of their holes.

"What on earth?" cried Karen who was the first to get there. "George! What have you done to your leg? It's bleeding!"

Owen came in, falling over a stool because his tramp hat was way down over his face, and Squeaky came panting up from the cellar. They all stood around and stared at George who thought he probably looked pale from his loss of blood and shock.

"It's nothing," said George with admirable carelessness, "just a scratch. But have I got news for you! I think I've found out who's been moving stuff around here. Letting out Shelby's animals and so on."

They crowded around and he told them about running into the man in the portrait and what a shock it had been.

"But how do you know it's the same man?" asked Monica. "Lots of men wear beards."

"It was his eyes," said George. "Golly! They gave you a grue—just to see 'em! Let me look at that picture again. I could swear it was the same man." As they all moved out into the hall toward the closet where the portrait was, he added, "And he looked at me as if he hated me—the same mean expression he has in the picture."

They went to the closet and George threw the door open. At first he thought the portrait was gone, but as soon as his eyes got used to the light he saw that it was still there. Although instead of the dark hateful eyes staring at them, there was only the yellowed back of the picture and the piece of broken rusty wire. Someone had turned the portrait to the wall.

10 "Who did that?" yelled George. Just after seeing the man in the portrait alive and walking around, it gave him a great shock. It was almost as if the man had come to life and stepped out of the picture.

Everybody said they had not touched the thing and then Karen said just what George had been thinking.

"See! There *are* ghosts, just like I said! That man you saw—he was a ghost. He lives in this picture except when he wants to walk abroad in the land"—Karen had been reading ghost stories for the last few months—"and then he takes human form and—"

"Oh, do be quiet!" cried Monica. "You're scaring

Owen silly! Look," she said, giving Owen a hard shove, "the man is still in the picture. It's nothing but a picture. I'll show you."

She walked into the closet and turned the big frame around. For a long moment the children stared and stared and then Owen began to cry. The canvas on which the portrait had been painted was gone!

Owen gave a wail like an injured wildcat and dashed for the front door. He knocked Squeaky off his feet and fell over Karen and dashed out to the porch, where he stepped on Snoopy's tail. Snoopy's yelps joined with Owen's bellow.

"Go after him!" George yelled. "Stop him! He'll go bawling home and blab the whole thing!"

Shelby ran after him and as soon as she could get out of the closet, Monica ran after Shelby.

Owen's hat was down over his eyes so it wasn't hard to catch him. But it was a lot harder to convince him that the man in the painting was not a ghost.

He refused to come back into the house and they all had to sit around on the porch and try to calm him down.

"Look," Monica said at last. "You know that picture of you Mamma has on her bureau?"

Owen nodded, snuffling.

"Well, that isn't *you* is it? It's just a picture. Now suppose somebody took the picture out of the frame and later somebody else saw you out playing. That wouldn't mean that you were a ghost, would it?"

Owen looked a little brighter as he thought about this, but not too happy.

"What I'd like to know is who the clown is who's doing all this funny business," said George. "We ought to stay around here and catch him."

"Maybe it's whoever owns the house. Maybe they want to get us out," said Karen.

"If they owned the house," said George, "all they'd have to do would be to tell us to get out. This is just some smarty trying to scare us."

"Probably one of our gang who didn't get in on the club," said Squeaky. "Somebody like Chuck Benson or Stuffy Alden."

"It could be a girl," said Monica.

"I don't think so. You notice everything happens at night," put in Shelby. "A girl wouldn't come around after dark."

"That's what you think," said Monica. "Girls are every bit as brave as boys."

"Hardee-hardee-hardeee-har!" said Squeaky rudely.

"You want to bet?" asked Karen, looking at him hard.

"Don't have to. Everybody knows girls are sissies."

"Hush up, you two," said George. "This isn't getting us anywhere. I move we all think about this and see if we can figure out who's doing this silly business and why."

"Yes—*why?*" said Monica. "There sure doesn't seem to be any sense to it. Anyway, we know it isn't a ghost.

Come on, let's go back inside. Karen and I are writing a play."

But Owen wouldn't budge. He just sat tight on the steps and shook his head.

"Look," Monica said at last, "we'll lock the silly old picture up in the closet. Then you can forget about it. Come on, I'll do it now."

But the closet had no key and although they looked all over the downstairs and the cellar they couldn't find one to fit the lock. Nor could they find the painted canvas. Finally Squeaky went down in the cellar and came back with an old rusty hatchet, a board, and some nails and boarded up the closet door.

"But he isn't in there," said Owen whose eyes seemed to have stretched in the last half hour. "He's outside somewhere."

"Oh, for the love of mud!" shrieked George. "There isn't any 'he.' Somebody wanted that picture—though heaven knows why—and they came and took it. They must have a key to this place. But the picture is not the man I saw downtown and the man was never in that picture. In the first place that picture was painted about a hundred years ago—maybe fifty. The man I saw would've been a baby then—I mean it couldn't be him, see?"

But Owen was not convinced and he wouldn't go into the house until Awful promised him he could bring his comic books and stay in the dining room.

"Just ignore him," Monica said to the others in a low tone. "He'll forget it."

Squeaky gave him part of an old candy bar and he curled up on some sofa cushions and read for the rest of the afternoon. The girls propped the door open into the pantry so that he could see them if he wanted to.

After that nothing mysterious happened for several days. They went about their work and stopped worrying about the man George had seen and the stolen picture. Awful made a beautiful rockery in one of Shelby's seed frames and Shelby found four baby lizards for it. They looked like alligators, climbing in and out of the water in the big abalone shell Monica had donated for a pool to the rockery, or sunning themselves on the specimens of quartz and mica and other stones. Karen found some ferns in the woods and planted them among the stones. The place was really pretty, like a miniature jungle. Shelby added the turtle he had bought at the dime store and Squeaky brought a baby minnow for the abalone pool.

Shelby's tadpoles were hatching into frogs and he put some of them in the rockery. Owen spent most of his time out in the yard catching flies and small beetles for the lizards.

Squeaky was trying to build a rocket. There weren't any helpful books at the drugstore and the school library was closed so he was experimenting with things he thought he remembered he had read about. Smells and smoke and an occasional weak *Pfff!"* came up from the cellar but so far nothing really dramatic had happened.

George was designing a plane that could do stunts—he hoped. And Awful was making a fine bug collection and had added a bat to his animals.

The girls were writing a play called *The Broken Hearts,* acted out every day with their dolls.

Some days the members brought their lunch and

stayed all day. The girls had learned to work the old electric stove and on rainy days they made soup or pancakes. They didn't all go every day because they had music lessons or had to go to the dentist or take typhoid shots or some other boring thing, but some of them were at the house part of every day except Sunday.

Then one morning they went into the house and all the furniture was changed around. The sofa which had been on one side of the room was pulled out into the middle of the floor. The chairs were in different places and all the drawers and cupboards were open— even the empty drawers in the bedrooms and the kitchen cupboards. Worst of all, the seed beds in Shelby's hothouse were all dug up. The lovely rockery was a mess. The other beds didn't matter much because they just had some plants in them for Raymond and a baby black snake to live in, but the rockery was something else.

Owen's hats had all been stuffed under the bed in his room. The only place that wasn't bothered was the long garden down the middle of the hothouse where Shelby had planted radishes and lettuce and carrots. Even the seed packages were still on the sticks at either end of the rows.

George was fit to be tied.

"This is the last straw," he yelled as he picked up one of his model planes from under a chair. "This has gone far enough. We've got to do something!"

"But what?" asked Karen. "Nobody ever does anything when we're around."

"Then we got to be around when they do," said Awful. "I move we come over here at night and see who's doing all this wacky business."

"It's worse than wacky," muttered George, holding up his precious plane and stroking it gently. "If he'd broken this it would've taken me weeks to redo it."

"How are we going to come here at night?" asked Monica. "You know they wouldn't let us. All of us would never be able to sneak out."

"I don't want to come," said Owen.

"You girls aren't coming and that's that," said George. "In the first place you'd get scared and probably start screeching if you saw a bat or heard a dog walking through the weeds. And in the second place girls just shouldn't be running around at night."

Monica looked as if she might swell up and burst, but before she could say anything Karen said, "I don't think we'd be scared, but I don't think we ought to hang around here at night."

George was surprised and Awful and Squeaky and Shelby looked as if they couldn't believe their ears. But they were relieved too. It would be a mess trying to hide out with two girls tagging along. It was going to be hard enough to keep four boys from being seen, especially when one was as fat as Squeaky.

"How'll we know what night he's coming?" asked Shelby.

"We won't," said George.

"No—we'll have to come every night till we catch him."

"What time?" said Squeaky. "We'll have to wait till the folks go to bed."

"Yeah, and that's pretty late in the summer," added Awful glumly.

"I have a better plan," said George. "Let's all say we're going to each others houses tonight—and so it won't be a lie, we will, but then we'll drift off to the clubhouse and see what we can see. We'll stay till about nine and then go home, huh? Let's just hope whoever it is comes before then."

"That'll be easy for me," said Awful. "My Dad and Mom play bridge tonight."

"My folks are having company so they won't miss me," said Shelby.

"I reckon I can get by with it," said Squeaky. "I'll think of something."

"Let's all meet at Shelby's barn about eight o'clock, shall we?" said George and they agreed on that."

The girls looked a little glum so George said, "You can do just as much as we do. If the folks get to wondering where we are you can alibi for us. Tell 'em you heard us talking of meeting over at Shelby's, see?"

"They won't ask me," said Monica. "But I won't give you away if I do happen to see anybody who wants to know."

So the meeting was all arranged. After they had finished tidying up, they left the clubhouse as Awful had to cut some grass and Karen had to take her music lesson and Owen wanted to go home anyway.

The path went through the woods, and while it was light enough it was awfully quiet and there was a lot of underbrush. George was halfway through and could hear the others talking just ahead of him when something made him turn quickly and look back. Someone was standing in the bushes not fifty feet in back of him.

The man had on a slouch hat pulled low over his face. He was in the shadow of a big pine, but George could have sworn that he had a beard and dark piercing eyes. In other words he was the man he had seen that other morning, the one in the painting. George ran on to catch up with the others. He had felt his scalp creeping just as it had when he had seen this sinister character before. He thought he knew now who had been breaking into the clubhouse—but why, he couldn't imagine. That was what he meant to find out.

11 🌿 George was so excited that night he could hardly eat supper, though there were biscuits and fried chicken, two of his favorite foods. He forced down two drumsticks and a second joint and two biscuits but could only eat one helping of dessert.

He was afraid his parents would notice how his appetite had failed, but Mr. Carpenter had just read a book on the modern short story and he and Mrs. Carpenter were discussing it.

Mrs. Carpenter did say once, "George, eat your lettuce," but then she went right back to arguing about somebody named Faulkner and somebody named

O'Hara. When his parents got on a subject like this they got as excited as if the fate of the nation depended on it.

If we yelled like that at each other, thought George, mixing his lettuce into his mashed potatoes so that he couldn't taste it, they'd send us away from the table.

But he was glad that his parents were so absorbed in literature because he could think about what he had to do that night.

He had decided to take some kind of weapon along for defense, but what, he didn't know. He thought of the wrench out in the garage. Just what he was going to do with it wasn't quite clear to him, but the memory of that dark disagreeable face and those penetrating eyes made George feel that if the man in the portrait was the one who was entering the house it would be a comfort to have some weapon.

It was still light at seven o'clock. George felt it would never get dark. He wandered around the yard and Karen trailed after him, asking all sorts of dumb questions like, "What'll you do if it is that man? If you see what he's doing, you still won't know why. Are you going to ask him?"

He left at a quarter of eight to get rid of her. He found Squeaky at the barn, sitting on the bench outside the door.

"I'm sure glad you're here," Squeaky said looking at the wrench George carried. "It's getting too dark now to sit around this spooky old barn by yourself. I wish the others would come."

"It's early," said George, sitting down by him. "Besides you can still see outdoors."

"But it's dark in there," said Squeaky, rolling his eyes toward the barn, "and rats or something's been stirring around right behind me."

"Here comes Awful," said George.

"Gosh!" complained Awful as he came through the yard. "I thought I wasn't going to make it. The Bakers are playing bridge with my folks and they wanted me to baby-sit with that dumb kid o' theirs, that Bobby. But I said I'd promised to help Shelby do something so they got Janey Pierce. Where's Shelby?"

"He'll be here in a minute I guess," said George. "I think we ought to have some kind of plan—I mean about what we're going to do when we get there."

"Yeah. Maybe we ought to divide up. Some of us watch the back and some the front."

"I don't know, Awful," said George. "Maybe we ought to stick together."

"Yeah!" Squeaky agreed. "If we get separated anything could happen."

Shelby joined them just then and they asked him what he thought.

"I think we ought to stick together, so we'll be able to tell who's who. Otherwise George might give one of us a sock with that wrench."

"You know the door in the front," said Awful. "It's got glass panels down the side. Suppose one of us looks in one panel—I mean two of us can look through those panels and two of us can take the front windows. Then either way he comes in or whether he goes, we can see him—you know, going from room to room."

"We'll have to hide behind that old swing till we know he's inside," said George. "Dark as it is tonight he won't see us unless he has a flashlight."

"He'll be using it to see where he's going—if he's got any sense," said Awful.

"We'll be ready to duck in case he starts to flash it around," said George.

Shelby showed them the flashlight he had brought. They agreed not to use it unless there was a real emergency because George said it would only betray their presence to the enemy.

It was dark in the woods but not so dark that they couldn't see the trees against the sky and the sandy path between the bushes. That is, until they got into the real woodsy part. Then it got so black they had to feel their way from tree to tree until they reached the open space right in front of the house.

"Wait!" whispered George. "Don't walk across the yard. If he's there he might see us. We've got to sneak around the sides of the clearing, real slow, so that he can't tell us from the bushes. Then we'll move up onto the porch, one at a time and take our places. Ready?"

"Ready," they mumbled and began to move in a wide circle toward the house.

When they got to the steps the porch looked as dark as the woods and they stood there together in the shadow of the shrubbery not really scared but not wanting to go on alone.

"You go first, George," said Awful.

"It was your idea," George said, stepping aside. "You go ahead and we'll follow."

"Are you crazy?" hissed Awful. "We'll all go. Come on, fellas. Stick close together."

Nobody wanted to be left in the dark shrubbery and nobody wanted much to go up on the porch alone. They moved together stepping on each other's feet. George held the wrench tight in his hand as if he expected to meet a dragon.

They had worn their sneakers and they hardly made any sound on the porch, but just as George was half way to the door something cold and clammy touched his hand. He all but fell down in a fit. He felt something bumping against his legs and then he realized that Snoopy had followed them. It made him feel a little better to know that Snoopy was there. Shelby knew it too and put his hand on the dog's head and whispered "Hi, boy. Be quiet now. Be quiet, hear?"

Snoopy thumped his tail on the porch, but it was a soft sound that a squirrel or a chipmunk might have made. The boys crept forward and after standing in front of the door a minute listening, they separated. Awful and Squeaky took the door panels and Shelby and George the windows. Snoopy went over and sat by Shelby. George wished he had a dog to be with him. It was awfully lonely and dark out there even if the window was just a few feet away from the door. Behind him was the open yard full of dim shadows and back of that the woods, black and full of all sorts of little sounds that could be something sneaking up on you.

Except for the whispering noises in the woods it was as quiet as all get-out. They stood there for what seemed like hours and nothing happened.

Finally George whispered, "Anybody know what time it is?"

"I got my watch." That was Squeaky. The watch had a luminous dial and George could see the faint eerie light, as Squeaky turned his wrist around and looked at it. "Twenty after eight," he said in a low tone.

"Good grief!" muttered George. And Awful said, "Gosh! I thought it was nine o'clock at least."

"Be quiet," said Shelby. "Half the town'll know we're here."

They went back to staring into the dark house. They couldn't see a thing except the faint gleam of a glass vase or a brass lamp reflecting what little light there was from the stars outside.

They waited for what seemed another hour or so, although Squeaky told them that it was only twenty minutes. And then, just as they were beginning to think this whole idea was crummy and stupid, something happened.

A faint light appeared at the top of the stairs. From the porch they could only see a short way up the stairs but there was a dim paleness there just like the sky before the sun really comes up.

Awful and Squeaky saw it first because the front door was opposite the stairs.

Awful said, "Pssst!" and waved his arm at George.

George and Shelby left the windows and they all stared through the door panes. There was no doubt about it there was a faint light on the stairs. The light wavered and bobbed around and then there was a strange metallic noise.

"Listen!" said George, and they all held their breaths.

There was a little more jangling and banging and then the light moved down the steps. It was plainly a flashlight and whoever held it had unlocked the iron grill at the head of the stairs.

"Jeepers!" breathed Squeaky. "He was upstairs all the time!"

"He's coming down!" gasped George.

The light was coming lower and lower. It was pointed toward the steps and behind it they could just see, not the figure of the man in the portrait, but a long grayish robe.

George was glad that Karen wasn't there. She'd have

had the screaming meemies and scared the Thing away. It did look pretty ghostly and George could hear one of the other boys draw in a sharp breath. Shelby whispered hoarsely, "Holy cats! A real ghost!"

The Thing had reached the bottom of the stairs now and turned toward the living room. They all tiptoed over to a living-room window. Snoopy, who knew something was up by this time, followed them and started to beat his tail on the porch floor. Shelby muttered, "Hush, dog!" and he sat still.

The light moved all over the room turning first to one thing and then another. If there's anything spookier than plain dark it's the sight of a flashlight beam moving around in that dark. Maybe it's because burglars and police use them or maybe it's just naturally weird-looking. It gave George the creeps.

Suddenly the Thing seemed to go crazy or the light did. It jerked and bobbed and flashed and wriggled, throwing the beam all around the room. Then it steadied and they saw what had happened. The Thing had held it in its hand while it picked up a rocking chair and set it on a table. The boys knew this because when it had done it, the Thing threw the light on the chair. There it sat, up on the table, rocking as naturally as you please, except that there wasn't anybody sitting in it.

"Well, I'll be!" said Awful, "what's the big idea of that?"

"Just to show us it's still around and can mess things up, I guess," said George.

The light moved over to a table across the room, then slowly traveled up to the big mirror that hung there. The beam made a sort of star on the old glass. The Thing stepped closer to the mirror and Shelby let out a gasping moan. Snoopy must have thought Shelby was hurt because he gave a growl and stood up, pushing under Shelby and putting his front paws on the window sill.

The Thing had lowered the flashlight and shone it on its face. That was what had made Shelby moan. For you could plainly see the ghost, or the vampire, or whatever it was in the mirror and it was enough to scare the daylights out of any living soul. The face was chalk white, with dark sunken eyes that looked as big as silver dollars. It had long jagged teeth and a blood-red mouth and flying around all this was a lot of wild gray hair.

The boys stood frozen for a moment and then Awful gave a bellow and turned and ran. Snoopy began to bark wildly and the Thing snapped around and shone the flashlight first on the window and then right on its face. It was even more hideous and frightening than it had looked in the mirror. George was petrified—if you can be petrified when your legs have turned to jelly. Shelby stepped back and onto one of Snoopy's paws. Snoopy stopped barking so he could howl and growl and Squeaky turned around and fell over George. All three scrambled up and ran, then fell down the front steps.

They started across the yard. When Awful, who was ahead of them, had reached the trees, he tripped on a rock. There was a loud thump and a groan and Shelby who was in the lead now stepped on Awful's stomach. Awful gave a scream that would have made a coyote sound like a mewing kitten and Shelby practically died of fright.

"Where's the flashlight?" yelled Shelby, who had been gripping it in his hand all the time. He turned it on Awful who was sitting up holding first his stomach and then his head. There was an enormous knot on the front of his head, and later Awful said he felt sick for two days afterward.

"Let's get into the woods!" said Squeaky. "That Thing can see us from the house!"

They hauled poor Awful to his feet and staggered into the woods with him. He kept groaning and moaning, and George, who was in the rear, kept looking back to see if they were being followed. Somewhere he'd lost the wrench but he wasn't going back for it. It was pitch black except up ahead where Shelby threw the beam from his torch. George couldn't have seen an elephant if he had been treading on its heels. That's why he practically scraped his ear off on a pine tree.

They stopped at Shelby's barn and sat down in the

back yard in the light from the house. Squeaky was shivering as if he'd been in a cold shower and Awful was still grunting and holding his head.

George felt sort of weak and his ear felt as if it were on fire. Shelby was the only one not hurt or scared to death, and he was out of breath.

After they shivered and panted and groaned for a few minutes, Awful said he had to go home and put something on his head, that he was going to bed and would probably die from Shelby stepping on his stomach.

"Maybe you better get a doctor," said Shelby nervously.

"Not me," said Awful, "I'm already trying to think up an excuse for this coconut growing on my head. If I had a doctor I'd have to tell everything, and I sure don't want to until we know just what's goin' on in that house."

Awful hadn't groaned all the time he was talking, so George knew he wasn't dying. He agreed that Awful ought to slip past the bridge players and go upstairs to bed.

"Put some liniment or something on that bump and a cold wash cloth," said Shelby. "Maybe it'll be almost gone tomorrow and they won't notice it."

"And if they do, say you bumped into a tree walking home," said George. "Which you did."

"Except I wasn't walking," said Awful with a sickly grin.

George's mind was still on the ghastly figure he had seen in the clubhouse, when he went upstairs to his room.

It was dark on the stairs and he hurried; anybody would have been a little nervous after what he had just been through. He didn't know just how nervous he was himself until Karen, barefooted and in her pajamas, jumped out at him from her room.

"Tell me! Did you see him? What happened?" she hissed.

George had fallen back against the wall and now he brushed a limp hand across his damp forehead. "For the love of mud! Don't ever do that again!"

"You mean I scared you?" asked Karen, delighted.

"You just don't know," said George weakly. "If you had been through what we've just been through—"

"Come into my room," said Karen, and pulled him inside and shut the door. "Now tell me. Gosh you're hot! And you've got a big scratch on your cheek. For heaven's sake, what happened?"

"If you'll stop yacking for a minute, I'll tell you," said George, sinking into an arm chair.

"You don't know," said George again and then told her the whole evening's adventure right from the beginning.

"I knew it was a ghost," said Karen, losing some of her pinkness. "I do believe there really are ghosts, and that's probably why nobody will live in that house. The place is haunted. Or else it was somebody wearing a

Halloween mask. Don't you remember Squeaky had one just like that last year—sort of tusks and eyes sunk in his head and all?"

"Yeah," said George slowly. "Gosh! I bet that was what it was!" He looked at his sister with admiration. Girls sometimes had what they call "feminine tuition," or something like that, he thought. "I bet that was old Blackbeard—the one in the picture—disguising himself. I bet he knew we were out there all the time. Maybe he's been there all the time too. He's just tryin' to run us off for some reason, the old coot!"

But even the most brilliant people can be wrong sometimes and George was just about as wrong as he could be about the Thing that had walked through the house and scared them off that night.

12 🌿 George had to take out the garbage next morning, and help Mrs. Sissom carry some glass jars up from the basement for preserving the last strawberries. But at last the club members all met over at Shelby's barn.

Awful told them that when he came downstairs that morning his mother nearly dropped the platter of scrambled eggs she was carrying and shrieked, "What in heaven's name has happened to you? Your face looks like an eggplant."

Awful was scared she might make him stay home, so he just tossed his head—which practically blinded him with pain—and said it was nothing. He had just run into a tree coming home last night.

His mother wasn't convinced, and she asked him if he'd been fighting again and he said no and could he have his breakfast because he wanted to mount some beetles right after he was through.

She said, "You can mount your beetles when you are through cleaning your room and taking out the garbage."

Awful said he knew then she wasn't going to get excited over the lump on his head, so he sat down and enjoyed his breakfast, though his stomach was still sore.

George said that it was good Awful's mother hadn't seen his ear or she would really have thought there'd been a fight. It was skinned, and swollen up like a sponge.

Monica was fit to be tied because she hadn't heard a word about what had happened the night before. Owen was wearing his Mexican sombrero so nobody knew what he was thinking. In fact, as Squeaky pointed out, if it weren't for his feet moving you wouldn't know he was there at all.

Monica agreed with George that it was the man in the portrait in deep disguise and that for some reason he wanted to scare them off the place.

"Maybe there's something valuable in the house and he's trying to find it," said Karen.

"Let him have it," said the sombrero.

"But why does he only come at night?" asked Karen. "If he isn't a ghost," she added.

"Because we're there in the daytime, silly," said George. "He wants to get rid of us, but he doesn't want us to see him. That's why he was all dressed up in that robe and that mask."

"If there's something valuable, let's look for it!" cried Monica.

"Yea, man!" said Squeaky. "Maybe it's a million dollars!"

"I bet it's hid in the chimney or around that fireplace!" said Shelby. "It's got something to do with that picture, I betcha."

"Maybe it was hidden behind the canvas," said Awful. "But if it was, why would he come back last night and be mooching around?"

"Maybe he didn't find it!" cried Karen. "Maybe we could!"

"I don't want it," mumbled Owen. "I think I'll go for a walk." The sombrero moved slowly out of the barn and down the driveway.

They watched it for a minute and then Shelby said, "Well—are we going over to the clubhouse or not?"

"Sure," said George, who thought maybe there might be something to this hidden-treasure theory. He remembered reading a story called *The Treasure of Ten-Tooth Ranch* in which a lot of gold and jewels had been hidden in an old saddle. Gosh! Suppose they found a lot of stuff like that in this house. Even if they couldn't claim it they might get a reward. And just finding it would be exciting. Anyway he'd like to beat old Black-beard to it, just for fun.

"I'll go," said Awful, "but if that chair's still rockin' or that picture is hangin' up all which ways again, I ain't gonna stay long!"

Everybody laughed and felt a little easier after that. In the daylight it was hard to imagine how terrifying things had been the night before. The woods were green and there was just enough breeze to make the leaves flutter. Birds and chipmunks moved about and an angry squirrel chittered at them from the very tree George had scraped his ear on.

But when they came to the clearing in front of the house they all stopped. No one wanted to go up on the porch first.

"You know something," George said in a low voice, "if that fellow was inside there last night and all the doors and windows were locked, maybe he's inside now."

"Oh, fiddlesticks," said Monica. "He could have a key same as us. Anyway, you've seen him outside twice— and the doors and windows were all locked then, re-member?"

"That's right," agreed George, feeling better. "Come on, let's go on in. He wouldn't do anything, probably, when we're all together."

They went up on the porch but they were careful not

to make any noise. George got the key and unlocked the door. They went slowly inside.

The hall was empty and so was the living room—that is, there was nobody there. What's more the rooms were tidy. The rocking chair was in place and from what they could see of the other rooms, everything was all right.

"I think you all made the whole thing up!" said Monica, walking into the middle of the living room and looking around. "What's that I smell?"

Squeaky sniffed. "It smells like cookies!" he said.

"It *is* cookies!" squealed Karen and ran over to the table under the mirror. There was a big yellow bowl full of delicious-looking cookies. She reached out to grab one.

"Don't!" cried George. "Maybe it's a trap. Maybe those cookies are poisoned or something."

Karen drew back her hand as if she had been stung by a wasp. Monica ran over, grabbed the bowl, and threw the whole thing out into the front yard.

"Stop!" cried Shelby. "Snoopy's out there!"

They rushed out onto the porch but it was too late. Snoopy was gulping down the cookies without chewing them, the way dogs eat, and before Shelby could reach him he had eated about a dozen.

"Oh, I'm so sorry!" wailed Monica. "What shall we do? Oh, dear, suppose he dies from them!"

"Relax," said George, "we don't know that they're

poisoned. That would be a pretty low-down trick even for an old grouch like Blackbeard."

"But what if he did—what if they are—suppose he—" stammered Monica who had turned as pale as a ghost herself. "We can't wait. I may have killed Snoopy!"

"Maybe we ought to take him to a vet," said Squeaky.

"There isn't one—not for miles," said Shelby.

"There's Doc Simpson," said Karen, and everybody turned to look at her.

Dr. Simpson was an old retired doctor who didn't practice any more except in an emergency. He liked dogs and the boys could see right off that Karen had a good idea.

"We'll take him," said Shelby to George. "The rest of you stay here. Come on, Snoopy old boy!"

"Poor old Snoopy!" said Monica, getting down on her knees and hugging him. "I didn't mean to hurt you."

Snoopy wriggled out of her arms and licked her all over the face, flapping that silly long tail of his and looking pleased to have so much attention.

"Let's get going," said Shelby, who looked worried. He and George started out with Snoopy lollaping along ahead of them certainly not looking very sick.

"Some poisons take a long time to work," Shelby said when George pointed this out. Shelby looked a lot sicker than Snoopy, and George was glad when they finally got to Doc's house back of what had once been an old mill. A stream ran through the yard and Snoopy stopped to take a long drink.

"Well, he can swallow," Shelby said.

"Of course he can," said George. "It's only with rabies they can't swallow and he's had the shots. He's thirsty after eating all those cookies."

"I read that some poisons make you awful thirsty," said Shelby.

George had never seen him look so gloomy and was relieved when they found Doc sitting on his porch behind the morning-glory vines, smoking his corncob pipe and reading a Western.

They told him they thought Snoopy had gotten hold of some poison. When he asked them how and when they had a hard time telling him without giving the secret of the club away.

Doc Simpson said rather crossly, "Well, I can't do much for him if I don't know what he got."

"We don't know," said Shelby. "It was some poisoned cookies—put out for the rats, we think. At least they were out in the yard and . . ." He couldn't think of anything more to say.

Doc looked over his glasses and said, "Hrrumph!" and stroked Snoopy's head.

"He doesn't look poisoned to me," Doc said. "Looks real happy and comfortable. Those cookies may just

have been dropped by somebody and they didn't want 'em after they'd been on the ground, or maybe they were stale and were just thrown out for the birds."

Just then Snoopy saw a squirrel and started after it. He chased it up a tree and stood there barking his silly head off.

"There's nothing wrong with that dog," said Doc, and went back to his rocking chair and his book.

"Whew!" said Shelby. "I sure am glad. Thanks, Doc."

George was glad too, as much because of Shelby as Snoopy.

They hurried back to the clubhouse and found that Awful and Squeaky had buried the rest of the cookies. Awful was mounting his beetles, Squeaky was working on his rocket, and the girls were making costumes for their doll soap opera. A mockingbird was singing its head off on top of an oak tree. Snoopy lay down under the rabbit hutches, where he stayed most of the time they were in the clubhouse. Everything looked peaceful and innocent, and it stayed that way all that day and the next.

In fact nothing much happened for almost a week. George was sure that he would get a threatening note in the mail. He could even see it, with the letters cut out of newspaper headlines:

StAY aWAy FrOM yoU KnOw WHere OR You'LL Be sOrrY!

Or that a mysterious voice would call one of them on the telephone. But no such thing happened.

The weather stayed good except for one or two days, and on those days they stayed inside and made cocoa and listened to Squeaky's transistor radio. Shelby's garden grew and they had lettuce with their sandwiches, when they brought their lunch. Squeaky's rocket was nearly finished and he was going to take it out into the clearing and set it off one day soon.

So much smoke and so many smells came up from the cellar where Squeaky was working that George said every time Squeaky came upstairs he expected to see him with horns and a tail and a pitchfork in his hand. Everybody seemed busy and happy.

It was better at home too. George overheard his mother talking to Mrs. Prentice. She said, "I suppose they're getting over the collecting stage. There isn't the clutter there used to be in their rooms. They seem to be outdoors all the time now, which is wonderful for them —and for me!"

Mrs. Prentice agreed. "Awful has gotten rid of a lot of his gruesome junk. I suppose the next thing is that they'll be wanting to drive the car, and will be getting interested in girls."

"Well, if they get interested in girls, at least they'll wash their necks and ears without our having to make them," said Mrs. Carpenter. That was all George heard. But it showed their idea had worked and that everybody was happy about it.

Then one day Awful and Shelby saw the man with the beard. He was standing in front of the post office, picking his teeth and looking up and down the street. Awful and Shelby knew right away who it was from the picture and from George's description. They hid behind a milk truck and watched him. After a while he threw away the toothpick and went into the post office. They waited until he came out and walked away.

They talked all the way home about what the man was doing in town, whether he was the one responsible for all the monkey business in the house, and whether he had put the cookies there—which seemed an odd thing for a man to do.

They stopped by George's house and told him what they'd seen. George was in the kitchen, having a peanut butter and jelly sandwich and a glass of Coke. They joined him and when they'd eaten, Mrs. Sissom asked them if they thought they could make it till lunch now. If so, would they please get out and let her mop the floor because they had tracked in dirt and dripped plum jelly. They took a couple of apples and a banana and said they guessed they could.

Out in the yard they sat down and talked some more.

"Maybe he doesn't have anything to do with the house," said Shelby. "Maybe he really isn't the man in the picture. Maybe we just think he looks like the picture because, well, because of the beard."

"George saw him in the woods, right outside the

house, remember?" said Awful. "I think the girls are right. He's looking for something in there, like an old will or some inheritance that was left to somebody else and he's trying to get it. And he comes at night because he never knows when we'll turn up during the day."

"There must be something crooked about it if he doesn't want anybody to see him," said George.

"Anyway, I thought we were going to look for it," said Squeaky.

"Yeah! We were, and then all the business about Snoopy and the cookies made us forget. Let's start now," cried Awful.

They looked for the girls and Squeaky and Owen, who had gotten over being so scared by now, and they all went over to the clubhouse. There was nothing out of place except Shelby's old terrapin. Shelby hadn't closed the hothouse door tight, and Cooter was crawling around in the front hall.

"We've already been through everything in the house —at least downstairs," Monica said.

"Well, we've got to look in unusual places," said George. "Like inside clocks and vases and for secret drawers and things."

They looked. They tapped walls and they turned over chairs and they even took up the rugs which was a big dirty job. They worked for three days and all they found was a lot of dust and dirt, an old fashioned side-comb with a few rhinestones in it, some buttons, an old pair of scissors, and several old letters that said, "Dear Ella, We got home all right and found a letter from John saying he was coming in March." Or, "Dear Jim, The brown suit came and fits real good. Mamma is well and is out planting tulip bulbs." All dull stuff about people they didn't know and not any of it interesting or exciting.

They finally gave up and decided that if there was anything that anybody wanted it had to be upstairs.

Awful decided to climb up on the porch roof and look in the upstairs windows. But the only room he could see into was empty. The other windows had little inside shutters that were slanted so that somebody inside could see out but you couldn't see in. Awful tried to open one window but it was locked and so he shinnied down the corner post on the porch, and they didn't know any more than they had before.

13 It was toward the last of July and hotter than all get-out. Squeaky had been working hard on his rocket and getting all nervous and cranky because so far it hadn't worked. He'd tried all kinds of chemicals, sugar, and gun powder which made a great bang but fizzled out before the rocket got a foot off the ground.

Finally he said he'd found the right formula. They were going to set it off on Tuesday morning. The girls brought ginger ale to toast its success, and a picnic lunch.

They all went out into the clearing in front of the house and stood around while Squeaky set up the rocket.

"I know this one is going to work," he said. He was so excited that he squeaked worse than ever. "And when I really perfect this, I'm going to make a missile and send white mice and things up in it."

"Not my mice," said Shelby, who was sitting beside Snoopy stroking his ears.

Owen had on his baseball cap and he turned it around backwards so he wouldn't miss anything.

Squeaky had an electric thingamajig that was to give out a spark and set the rocket off. Everybody sat down in a circle and Squeaky stood in the middle. After fiddling around for what seemed like a couple of hours, he said, "O.K. Watch out!" and started the countdown. He'd just gotten to seven when the rocket made a noise like a steam engine, spluttered, and shot up into the air. Everybody looked up with their mouths open. The rocket gave a twist and then came down. But not on the ground. It shot through one of the upstairs windows, glass and all.

There was just a second of silence and then a crash and then the whole house seemed about to go to pieces. Snoopy howled and took off for the woods. There was a scream and the sound of doors being slammed, a rattling of chains, and a shriek.

The club members sprang up and stood still for a second—with their mouths still open in surprise. Then George sprinted toward the house and the others followed.

There was a smell of sulphur in the hall but no other damage they could see. What they did see was a little old lady sitting on the bottom step of the stairs, holding her head. She glared at them with an indignant expression for a moment and then started to get up.

Monica and Karen both ran up to her. Monica said, "Wait! Don't move! Are you hurt? Did you fall down the stairs?"

"Oh, dear!" moaned Karen while the old lady, rubbing her backside said, "Fiddlesticks! I'm not that old and fragile. Besides, I didn't fall. I just stumbled on the last two steps."

She walked across to the living room and sat in the big overstuffed chair. She looked at Squeaky.

"That was some rocket," she said with a grin. Squeaky turned red in the face. "I suppose you had powdered zinc? And potassium sulphate?"

Squeaky was too astonished to answer. He just nodded, his eyes as big as they could get—which isn't too big because he's so fat.

"You see, I have a lot of time to read," she said, "and I'm interested in a lot of things."

"Have you been here all the time?" Monica asked.

"Was it you who did all those things like taking the picture out of its frame, and everything?"

"I took the picture," she said, "but I don't know about other things. Oh, yes, I left you some cookies. I hope you liked them."

The club members looked at each other with various expressions of embarrassment. Monica said, "Oh, y-yes —they were wonderful. We thank you."

"Then you didn't let all my animals out?" asked Shelby.

"That must have been that mean old J. T.," said the old lady. "J. T.'s my cousin," she explained. "We're the only two Spears left," she added. "I'm Delphine. This house belonged to our uncle, Old J. T., and when he died he left it to me. He'd been in a rest home for months, that's why it's so dusty and all. He lived here a long time by himself and a man alone just don't keep things up."

"Who was the picture of, and what happened to it?" asked Karen.

"It was Old J. T. He was as mean as poison and I just got tired of looking at it. I cut it up into little pieces."

"But he gave you this house," said Monica. "He couldn't be all mean."

"For spite," said Miss Spears. "He planned to leave it to my cousin but somebody wrote and told him they'd seen J. T. out West and that he was gambling and drinking." Miss Spears lowered her voice and drew in her chin in horror. "Old J. T. always thought gambling and drinking were unforgivable! So he didn't leave him anything, though he always said he would leave him everything he had in the world."

"But that wasn't right!" cried George. "He should have left him *something*."

"I know," said Miss Spears, looking embarrassed. "Not that J. T. needs a house—he's a foot-loose bachelor still, I guess. But I felt it was wrong and I was scared."

"Scared? Of what?" asked Karen.

"Of J. T. He was a mean boy and I knew he'd be a mean man, though I haven't seen him in years. I didn't want him to know I was living here. That's why I moved upstairs. But even then I thought he might do something real hateful—like burning the place down, or hurting me in some way. That's why I was glad when you all moved in."

George and Shelby looked at each other. Now it was their turn to be embarrassed.

"We shouldn't have barged in like this," said George. "But we did need a clubhouse."

"I know." Miss Spears nodded. "I heard everything you said the first day or so. After that I just enjoyed knowing you were down here. You see, I felt sure J. T. wouldn't do anything to me with all you children around. The nights were bad though."

"He always came at night," said Shelby. "That's

when he let out my animals and knocked the picture upside down and all."

"Yes, I know. He broke in somehow. I was scared stiff all the time!" cried Miss Spears. "Then one night I thought I heard him and I went down to scare him—"

"Wearing that awful mask!" cried George.

"Yes. He couldn't swear it was me behind that. I knew what a coward he was. Why he was scared of cows when he was little!"

"But it was us you scared!" Squeaky cried, laughing wheezily.

"Yes. I was sorry about that. That's why I made the cookies."

The children looked embarrassed again, especially George who had been the one to suggest that the cookies were poisoned.

"I would have made them sooner, only I had a hard time slipping out and getting groceries and I needed some of those little chocolate things."

"How *did* you get in and out?" asked Karen. "We had the key."

"I didn't go very often," said Miss Spears. "I didn't miss the key for several days. I nearly died when I realized I must have left it in the lock. Then when I went down it was gone and the door was locked. I was sure that J. T. had it. But I climbed out one of the windows onto the porch and I looked everywhere for it. And I found it!" she ended triumphantly. "After that whenever I came back from shopping I just got the key, opened the door, carried in my groceries, locked the door, then went out the window, put the key back and came in and shut the window. See?"

"I'm glad you liked the cookies," she added as the children sat staring at her in astonishment. "I put extra chocolate and nuts in them."

Squeaky groaned. To think what he had missed! He gave George a dirty look. George said hastily, "But, Miss Spears, are you going to stay here? You can't stay upstairs always, afraid of J. T."

"I'd like to. I loved Aunt Jessie, Old J. T's wife. I had many happy summers here in this house as a child. But it needs a lot of repairs and then there are the taxes. I just have a room in town, but I don't know whether I could finance a house like this."

"Oh, I hope so!" said Karen. "This house needs somebody just like you to live in it and take care of it."

"We'll move out," said George unhappily.

"Not at all," said Miss Spears. "The upstairs is plenty big enough for a nice apartment. I like having you here. And just since we've been talking I thought of something. My dear friend, Eloise Evans, has been begging me to take an apartment with her. She'd pay half the expenses, see? Maybe this is just the place for us. Her share would help pay the taxes. But it will be a hard row to hoe—especially making repairs."

"What does your cousin J. T. look like?" George asked suddenly.

"Just like that picture of Uncle J. T." said Miss Spears sharply. "That's one reason I couldn't stand it."

"Well, what about him?" asked Shelby. "What about J. T. He'll still be around."

"Yes—what about J. T.?" said a deep voice from the doorway.

Miss Spears gave a weak scream and fell back in her chair. Her face was as white as the mask she had worn that dreadful night.

Striding into the room came the man in the picture. He looked angry and mean and the children wished they could be swallowed up by a large hole in the floor. Owen gave a moan and flew behind a curtain. Karen and Monica clutched each other fearfully.

"A fine thing!" said the man, sitting down on an over-stuffed chair that was bursting its cover in a dozen places. "You've got those kids thinking I'm a criminal, or something."

"Wh—wh—what do you want?" asked Miss Spears weakly. "I'll give you the house. Just don't do anything mean."

"Why, I wouldn't have this dusty old firetrap!" cried J. T. "You're welcome to it and its leaky roof and rusty pipes. I don't want a thing but Uncle Jethro's watch—the one that chimes—and those two old blue onion-patterned platters. Where are they?"

"Upstairs," said Miss Spears hastily. "I'll get them."

She started to get up, but he leaned forward and pushed her back into her chair.

"We can get them later. I've wanted that watch for thirty years. Uncle Jethro used to take it out and make it chime for me when I was knee-high to a grasshopper. He always said he'd give it to me someday."

"Well, I'm sure you're welcome to it," said Miss Spears primly. She added, "but what do you want the platters for?"

"I always liked them too," said J. T., grinning. When he grinned he looked very nice—not mean at all.

"Aunt Jessie used to serve fried apples on one—remember?—and sausages on the other. As a boy I thought there was nothing better in this world. I still do. I'd just like to have them if they're still here."

"Yes, they are. Upstairs, like I said. You're welcome to them."

"I just wish my wife could learn to fry apples the way Aunt Jessie did."

"*Your wife?*" cried Miss Spears, sitting up quickly. "You're married?"

"Yes, the devil has a wife," said J. T., laughing. "We live in Georgia, down on the coast. What's more I have two children, a boy and a girl. And I don't beat 'em, or eat 'em."

"Why didn't you just come to me in the first place?" demanded Miss Spears, her courage returning now that J. T. seemed to be human after all.

"I knew you hated me. I guess I was mean as a kid," he added. "But I looked so much like Uncle Jethro that everybody thought I *was* like him. The truth was I was just plain scared most of the time. I was an awful coward," he said, turning to the club members. "I was even scared of cows. They have such big eyes. And those horns! I acted mean to hide how scared I was. But I've gotten over that. Anyway, I thought you wouldn't give me the back of your hand, so I tried to get in and find the things for myself. Then these kids kept coming here so I didn't feel safe in the daytime. I tried to scare 'em off at night."

"What a ridiculous kettle of fish!" cried Miss Spears. "I would have gladly given you anything in the house —to get rid of you," she added, blushing a little, but laughing.

Owen crept out from behind the curtain and went and leaned on her knee.

"I like you," he said.

"Bless you!" cried Miss Spears. "I like you too. And I tell you what, Owen. I have my granddaddy's Civil War hat upstairs in a trunk and I'll give that to you the very next time you come over."

"Gosh!" said Owen overwhelmed. "Thanks, Miss Spears."

"We've got to go," said George suddenly. "But we'll be back and maybe—" he looked at Miss Spears as if he were bursting with some big idea, "—maybe we'll have some good news for you."

"Sorry about all I did to upset you," said J. T., putting out his hand to George.

George shook it and mumbled something and the Collectors' Club hurried out of the house in a body.

They had no sooner gotten across the clearing than Awful said, "What was the idea of telling her we'd be back with news for her?"

"I had a swell idea," said George. "remember she's worried about the repairs and taxes?" The others nodded. "Well, I think we ought to help her."

"How, for Pete's sake?" cried Awful. "I haven't had any allowance for weeks."

"And none of us has much," said Monica. "What good would twenty-five cents apiece do her?"

"Naw, it wouldn't pay for the lights and water we use," said Squeaky.

"Do you mean help her with money?" asked Karen. "Or just doing things for her?"

"Both," said George, who hadn't thought of the "doing things" part before. "What I thought of was this. We'd tell our parents"—a chorus of groans went up— "and remind 'em how much they like having our junk out of their houses and that Miss Spears really likes to have us there. Then maybe they'd be willing to pay her for letting us use the downstairs."

There was a stunned silence after this as each member of the club thought over how his or her parents would react. They recalled how much neater their rooms were since they'd had the club, and suddenly a look of delight spread over each face.

"I bet they would!" cried Karen. "It wouldn't be much if each family chipped in and I bet they'd think it was worth it."

"Me too," said Awful. "When'll we tell 'em?"

"Let's ask 'em to get together tonight," said George. "I'll do the talking or they'll never get the straight of it—I mean, if we all start gabblin' at once. I bet that just two or three dollars a month apiece will be enough for that old house. I know Dad will pay it because I've heard him say a dozen times it was too bad the kids around here had no place to gather."

"That's what Mother says," said Monica. "You know, George, I believe they'll go for it."

Monica was right. The grownups did "go for it" and after the first shock of surprise were delighted with the whole arrangement. The fathers gladly agreed to pay a small sum for "rent" and the mothers came over and helped the club members clean and tidy the whole house.

Mrs. Sissom was called in and Monica's mother brought her yard man. In a week they had everything shipshape and shining.

Miss Spears was in a perfect frenzy of excitement.

The day after her friend Miss Evans moved in, she gave a party for the club members and their parents.

Miss Spears, wearing a becoming blue dress, and looking ten years younger, served pink lemonade. Miss Evans passed plate after plate of cookies, and the Collectors' Club and their parents laughed and jabbered and dashed back and forth as if they had known Miss Spears always. The fathers made a tour of the club quarters, just as parents do on parents' night at school, and agreed that the house looked lovely in spite of still being shabby.

In a very impressive ceremony, Owen, wearing Miss Spears' grandfather's Civil War cap, presented her with a large painting of bright flowers. The club had pledged their allowances for the next six weeks to pay for it. The picture had been put into the frame that sour-looking Uncle J. T. had been in. George made a speech about how much they appreciated Miss Spears' letting them stay and everybody applauded.

Squeaky had made a rocket for the occasion and the party gathered outside to watch it go off. He had named it Delphine for Miss Spears, and it went straight up as far as you could see. He never found it and Squeaky said, which was true, that you couldn't prove that Delphine wasn't now on the moon. They drank ginger ale to toast its success, and everybody was very happy.

ABOUT THE AUTHOR

CHRISTINE GOVAN has been winning readers and critical acclaim for her children's books for over thirty years. Mrs. Govan was born in New York City, but moved to Tennessee at the age of four. After attending the University of Chattanooga she taught school, and has been a regular reviewer for the *Chattanooga Times*. Many of her earlier books, among them *Number 5 Hackberry Street*, *Willow Landing*, *The Delectable Mountain*, and *Return to Hackberry Street*, re-create the special atmosphere and variety of life in the South at the turn of the century.

Mrs. Govan is married to Gilbert Govan, an author, Civil War historian, and former librarian, and they now live on Lookout Mountain, Tennessee. The Govans' two daughters, Emily and Mary, are both established writers, and their son, James, is librarian at Swarthmore College in Pennsylvania.